The Milky Way

To Geneviève

The Milky Way

A Novel

Louise Dupré

Translated by
Liedewy Hawke

SIMON & PIERRE
A MEMBER OF THE DUNDURN GROUP
TORONTO · OXFORD

Editor: Shirley Knight Morris
Design: Jennifer Scott
Printer: Transcontinental

National Library of Canada Cataloguing in Publication Data

Dupré Louise, 1949–
 [Voie lactée. English]
  The Milky Way

Translation of: La voie lactée.
ISBN 1-55002-383-7

I. Hawke, Liedewy II. Title. III. Title: Voie lactée. English.

PS8557.U66V6513 2002   C843'.54   C2002-901069-1
PQ3919.2.D849V6513 2002

1   2   3   4   5   06   05   04   03   02

Canada🍁

THE CANADA COUNCIL | LE CONSEIL DES ARTS
FOR THE ARTS | DU CANADA
SINCE 1957 | DEPUIS 1957

ONTARIO ARTS COUNCIL
CONSEIL DES ARTS DE L'ONTARIO

We acknowledge the support of the **Canada Council for the Arts** and the **Ontario Arts Council** for our publishing program. We also acknowledge the financial support of the **Government of Canada** through the **Book Publishing Industry Development Program** and **The Association for the Export of Canadian Books**, and the **Government of Ontario** through the **Ontario Book Publishers Tax Credit** program.

Care has been taken to trace the ownership of copyright material used in this book. The author and the publisher welcome any information enabling them to rectify any references or credit in subsequent editions.

J. Kirk Howard, President

Cover Photo: Geneviève Cadieux, *La Voie lactée*, 1992 light box: 183 x 457 cm
Collection of Musée d'art contemporain de Montréal
Photo credit: Louis Lussier
Courtesy of Galerie René Blouin, Montréal

Printed and bound in Canada.♻
Printed on recycled paper.

www.dundurn.com

Dundurn Press	Dundurn Press	Dundurn Press
8 Market Street	73 Lime Walk	2250 Military Road
Suite 200	Headington, Oxford,	Tonawanda NY
Toronto, Ontario, Canada	England	U.S.A. 14150
M5E 1M6	OX3 7AD	

Every encounter with the truth
Will lead us from our opened graves
Outside into the light

Lalla Romano

table of contents

Part I

1

The city again. A loud, leaden jumble. It filters down into my inner ear, and all I hear now is a woman's scream that shakes the concrete before dying away against the rail of my balcony. I feel like screaming even louder than the city. I didn't want to come back. The luggage is waiting near the front door, the plants need watering, a film of dust covers the furniture, and there's the mail. Circulars, bills I need to pay right away. After that, I must listen to the string of messages on the answering machine. Then I'll have to call the office.

I didn't want to come back. I haven't come back. No. I am still in Tunis, clinging to a phrase, to the kind of question men sometimes ask when they are no longer of an age to make demands. *Will I see you again, Anna?* I could have replied curtly, *Don't call me Anna.* But I answered, *Yes, Alessandro,* and I added, *Definitely,* in order to convince myself, no doubt. The word *yes* is so hackneyed it doesn't commit us to anything any more. We need to reinforce it, pile one word on top of another, chain them together, we add things on, we explain, sometimes we repeat ourselves. Or we strain our voice. I only whispered, though, emphasizing slightly, yes, we would see each other again. I haven't come back yet. I am in the arms of a man I don't know.

Where will we see each other again, Alessandro Moretti — in Rome or in Carthage? Not here. No, not here. Already a cool wind creeps in beneath one's hair, and the nape of the neck is open to its bite. A long shiver runs up our spine, we wrap our arms tightly around ourselves, we try to protect ourselves. Our breath will soon send plumes into the air, the cold will deaden buildings and trees. Then it will seize the river, in the distance, and the ships will leave for summer seas. You would never get used to this cold, which lies in wait for us on winter nights, even when we are asleep. I have never got used to it. I often dream about a wilderness of ice, about a glacial light, or the wolves from my childhood howling in my bedroom, that relentless struggle for survival. Would you find me desirable, Alessandro, in my ankle-length down coat, my hair hidden away beneath a schoolgirl's tuque? And with that scarf covering my cheeks when the wind blows so fiercely people hunch their shoulders against it?

I will join you in Carthage. I will drop off my luggage at my hotel in Tunis, then take the local train. I will absorb every detail of the landscape all the way to the tiny station that sits right in front of the ruins. I'll stride along beneath the clear blue sky, in the afternoon, alone on the deserted streets. I'll continue walking with my white skin, my winter skin. Soon the Roman city will appear, the heaps of stones, that injured matter displayed before our voyeuristic eyes. *Have you never felt as though you were desecrating tombs, Mr. Moretti?* You laughed when I said that. I didn't blush. I really did ask myself that question. Who could have answered it better than you? Haven't you been in charge of the excavations at Carthage for thirty years? You didn't seem offended. You kept on walking along the path of scorched earth that led to the bus which was waiting for us, then you suddenly turned around to face me and said with a smile, *One has to be a profaner to do this job.*

The bus drove at an alarming speed along the road back to Tunis. It overtook dilapidated cars, trucks loaded with live-stock, a few tractors returning to the farm after a hard day's work. But I wasn't afraid of dying there, on that badly paved road. You were telling me about your work, the disembowelled earth, the strata of red earth protecting its mysteries, and the patience, the infinite patience required — one has to look, dig, interpret, sift, put the fragments back together like the pieces in a puzzle. You labour away stubbornly, you're looking for a lost piece, you keep hoping. Sometimes a vase is almost intact, then you are in a state of grace.

I followed you all the way to the hotel bar without asking you if it was all right. That conference was suddenly pointless, our minds were filled with the red earth of Carthage, we were descending together into the private places where the Romans lived their lives, and the Phoenicians before them. You wanted to take me to that little restaurant whose owner you knew. He was a cousin. I asked a naïve question. *Aren't you from Rome, Alessandro?* Your silence hung heavily in the jasmine-scented air. Then you replied, *My wife was Tunisian.* You didn't elabo-rate, you led me once again deep into the red earth of the past. You erected an impenetrable wall to protect your life.

You didn't talk to me about her either during the meal or while we were having our coffee. Just this one sentence, uttered in a solemn voice as we were leaving, *I hadn't been here since*

Jasmina's death. I lowered my eyes, ashamed and relieved. We walked back to the hotel. I will always remember everything I saw during that walk — the illuminated boulevard, the flower stalls, strollers sipping mint tea at sidewalk cafés, the pitch-black sky dotted with barely visible yellow specks. You pointed out a side street, murmuring, *That's where we lived when the children were small.* Then you slipped your arm through mine. A discreet, desperate gesture, as when someone revisits, for the first time after a break-up, a place where they once loved.

Neither of us suggested we have one last drink. You followed me down the corridor to my room. I stopped in front of a brown door, similar to all the others. As usual, I had to empty out my handbag to find my key. You waited patiently. Then you turned to go, without asking if you could come in. You simply said, *Thank you.* I'm the one who stepped forward to kiss you, so my lips would leave a trace in your grey beard. You hugged me tightly, you looked deep into my eyes and said with a laugh, *Anna Martin, Alessandro Moretti. We both have the name of a drink.* I didn't react. Once again, I let you call me Anna.

2

The mountain is almost impossible to see. You can just barely distinguish its outline through the haze. It seems to be floating in space, a diamond, a cone, an ice floe that had slipped over the clouds and, for some unfathomable reason, come to a stop here. The river, too, is hidden — no boats, with flags you might recognize. It flows gloomily along through the misty landscape to the gulf, where its grey waters will be swallowed by the sea. In one corner of the window there's a lighter patch, growing larger, trying to assert itself. Before the end of the afternoon, the sun will have managed to break through, and the city will be bathed in its familiar Sunday light.

Everything is quiet, the quiet perfection of Sundays. It should take about an hour to go through the messages I received during my absence, write a few letters, tidy up my desk. I am putting things in order. I am settling back into my old life. Then Jean-Bernard will arrive, and Dominique and Maria, Marc probably too — they will all be here, the office will be filled with its usual Sunday gaiety. Dominique will say, *What are you doing here!* Jean-Bernard or Marc will reply, *I've got tons of work to do.* They'll go one better, give details, but no one will admit, *I wanted to get away from the Sunday blues.*

Here's Jean-Bernard already. He kisses me, lets out a whoop. I look better, so he says. Then he drops into the armchair in front of me. *Now tell me all about it.* So I have to tell him. About Tunis, the conference, the latest trends in architecture. I get caught up in the story, I describe design shifts, I make a drawing on the back of a memorandum. Jean-Bernard comes closer, puts his finger on the sketch. I draw other lines which quickly turn into houses, I take out more paper, and on it goes. Yes, it was a wonderful conference. I'll give an overview of it tomorrow for the others. Next year it will be in New York, we should all go.

Now the sun has pierced the clouds, a ship glides slowly over the satiny surface of the river. I point it out to him — a buoyant spontaneous gesture, a last trace of childhood days re-emerging, as they sometimes do when I feel joyful, in unguarded moments. What has happened while I was away? I ask the question out of politeness. What unusual event could possibly have taken place in an architects' office during an ordinary week in November? Jean-Bernard is going to get his cigarettes, I am entitled to a full report. The steamer is no longer visible on the surface of the river, water specks shimmer peacefully in the window's rectangle, they will shimmer until new boats come into view. Greece, England, or an unknown pennant. In that case I'll open my dictionary at the page where I've put a bookmark. I'll examine illustrations of the flags and check off the one flapping in front of me. For one brief moment I will be a captain, I'll sail away, I'll go and join Alessandro in Rome.

That lingering sadness in your eyes. Jean-Bernard plops himself down into the armchair in front of me again. *You worry me*. I really should try to look like a woman who is just back from a trip, a happy, relaxed, refreshed kind of look. If only I could spread my lips, as though to say, *I'm all right*. But there's a short-circuit in my head and the words take shape by themselves, without my consent. I talk about Alessandro Moretti, I talk about Carthage, I talk about archaeology, I say, *I wish I hadn't come back*. Jean-Bernard stares at me, dazed. Then there is silence, nothing but this endless silence hovering over the patch of sunlight between us on my desk. Jean-Bernard lights another cigarette, slowly begins to smile. I try to smile too, but I simply can't.

A few snowflakes whirl around in the November sky, the first ones probably. I watch them, and I see empty Sundays, then empty Christmas holidays, empty vacations, the emptiness of time. I think about Alessandro Moretti in Rome, alone too, I'm sure. Love never happens at the right moment.

3

Already an inky darkness hangs over the city, an inescapable gloom. It's all very well to join the others at a lecture, then crowd into a bar with them, sink your lips into the golden foam of a beer, but sooner or later you have to go home. To accept the darkness. *Can I drop anybody off?* Jean-Bernard will always ask the same question. I often walk home. I turn up the collar of my coat, kiss everyone goodnight, and dash out. I let myself be swept along by the flood of languages. In the bright light from shop windows and street lamps, they blend into a single buzz, a single weariness. This is Babel, the people of Babel. There are dozens of towers here, but they don't incur God's wrath. They're probably too low, on a human scale. People aren't trying to reach heaven — all they want is wine on the table, some peace and quiet, a good night's sleep before facing the next day's struggle.

With a hurried hello to a neighbour in the lobby, I step inside the elevator, press sixteen while searching for my keys. Without taking off my coat, I run into the bedroom, turn on the computer. Yesterday there was no message from Alessandro, but had he really got back home? The screen lights up. In a few moments I'll be confronted with the truth. Three messages today, the last one is from Rome. My jaw relaxes, so do the muscles at the back of my neck. I breathe in, I'm able to breathe normally. To take off my coat, throw it on the bedspread.

When will we see each other again, Anna? That's all the message says. When will we meet again? At Christmas, Easter, next year, or in ten years? It doesn't matter, we'll meet again. We will, Alessandro, I know it now — we've entered a continuum. Time will no longer twist around itself. We have a history. There is something to look forward to, our eyes turned towards the large numbers on the calendar. I will start dreaming once again about a man's hands on my body. Your slow, tender gestures, Alessandro. I so desperately want to dream.

Let's meet as soon as possible. I click *Send*, I try to follow my sentence's journey all the way to you. I can see you smile, you slowly repeat all the words, you translate them into your own language. *Let's meet as soon as possible.* Just an ordinary sentence, yet it asks without imploring, it conjures up a smile, a caress in the small of the back. It inspires plans to outwit loneliness, perhaps a first confession, *I love you, Anna.* I will let you call me Anna. I have almost forgotten it is my aunt's name.

Migratory birds — we live in the age of the big migratory birds. That's what you said at the airport just before takeoff. We were surrounded by architects, also on their way home. We would all meet again at another conference, in a year, or in five years, and we would wonder, *Where have we met before?* Then a gesture would come back to us, or a conversation at break time, about work, sometimes about the children, and all of a sudden the person in front of us would emerge from the background, they would have a soul of their own, a life of their own. But at the airport nobody spoke, nobody moved, we were all rigidly waiting.

The night before, a plane had plunged into the Mediterranean, two hundred and sixty passengers, no survivors in spite of the search efforts. A woman nonchalantly crossed her legs, showing a tiny bit of lace from her slip. A man had been reading the same page of his newspaper for the last half hour. Yet no one would have admitted they were afraid. I got up with Alessandro when the flight to Rome was announced. I followed him right up to the gate, took his hand in mine and held it for a long time without saying a word. Anything I might have said would have sounded ridiculous, like a second-rate movie you rent on certain nights when you're not in the mood for truth.

Alessandro was the brave one. He lifted my hand up to his lips and I felt his soft skin against mine. I watched him as he slowly walked away. Then I went back to sit with my fellow architects. Two more hours of waiting. Our flight had been delayed. But strangely enough, I wasn't afraid any more. No, I wasn't.

4

First, a barely noticeable sensation of giddiness, then a real dizzy spell, the city will begin to turn like a merry-go-round, faster and faster, and gradually everything merges into a single endless torment, an open mouth letting out a silent scream. I force my eyelids to come unstuck. Everything is quiet and black, a muddy kind of black — the chest of drawers, the book-case, the china cats on top of the bookcase, the computer. I push my pillow against the head of the bed, stare at the unlit computer which is blind to the muddy blackness. I must take deep breaths until my heart beats in unison with the night, until I've stemmed the rush of time and returned to the peace of my bedroom.

That nightmare again. How many nights, or weeks, or months will it take for the woman's lips to fade? She was smiling, she smiled at me, I'm sure of it, she was smiling, graceful in her fall. And perhaps she was still smiling when she crashed down on the busy sidewalk. While I stood, paralyzed, on my balcony, looking straight ahead of me, at the river, the rectangle of the river between two buildings. I was searching for a ship that could take me away to the sea.

A vertical streak against the dirty blackness, a paler gloom. Daybreak is near, I won't be able to go back to sleep.

I'll go to work yet again with eyes that reveal my sleepless night, and Jean-Bernard will say to me, *You've had your nightmare again.* For the twentieth time I'll go over my story. How I came home with a bag of groceries. In the elevator, the woman talked to me — she had never spoken to me before — she seemed calm, almost joyful. It was the first beautiful evening in May. I got out on the sixteenth floor, *Have a nice evening*, while she continued on up. Then the usual homecoming gestures. I put a symphony on the CD player, poured myself a beer, got the vegetables ready for the salad, wiped the balcony table with a damp cloth. I sat down in the orangey glow of twilight and watched the city, moving slowly. Pedestrians, the size of pinheads, chatting while they crossed the boulevards. Seagulls, soundlessly gliding towards the water. Then a sudden vision. The woman, the woman's smile, the woman's open arms, the woman's smiling eyes when her gaze met mine, I'd swear to it. For one brief moment she soared as she fell, her arms like wings. What were you doing at that very instant, Alessandro?

Not even once did I have that nightmare during my trip. In the fragrant Tunisian air one can't imagine that a woman might want to end her life. Over there, one believes in a peaceful death, the body quietly returning to the wisdom of the earth. That's how you see things, Alessandro. *My wife passed away in a room in that hospital.* You pronounced these words in your grave voice. I swivelled around so I might carry that image back with me, but the hotel bus was driving too fast, trying to get us to the airport on time, it seemed. It wasn't me who asked you what she had died of, but an architect from France. I strained to overhear, *Cancer*. You'd met her here at the time of your first excavations. Thirty-five years of marriage. Two sons, one in Rome, the other in Florence. I looked intently at the scenery. A fine layer of dust tinged the road with gold, my heart was pounding away. And my temples throbbed. Jealousy. I was jealous of a dead woman who could have been my mother's sister.

How about you? Now the French architect turned his attention on me. Me? No husband, no children, but an ever-growing number of houses, and recently that school to renovate, a present from a colleague, Jérôme Langlois, who had taken it into his head to vanish into the cold thin air of February, almost three years ago. A light touch on my shoulder, Alessandro's hand. I must have been talking a little bit fast, as when you are trying to free yourself from blame. I fell silent and returned to the dusty landscape. No husband, no children, but a father, a mother, lovers, of course, a fine collection of lovers neatly filed away in my memory, and my colleagues at work — Maria, Marc, Dominique, Jean-Bernard. Spare-time activities, too — skiing in winter, the beach in summer — a lot of drive, a capacity for seeing far into the future, at least until that evening in May when my soul crashed down on the busy sidewalk. But that's not something one says to an architect one is speaking to for the first time. To you I might, Alessandro, if we are lucky enough to meet again.

The French architect carried on with the conversation, he started to talk about twenty-first-century design, and you responded, Alessandro, you agreed with him, you really seemed to be interested in what he was saying. I couldn't tell if you were. I hardly know you. The ruins at Carthage, a meal at a restaurant owned by your wife's cousin, just a few fragments from your life. But you want to see me again — that determination is there, clasped tightly in the palm of my hand. And I need a determination like yours, Alessandro, a will more stubborn than mine.

5

A holy moment. A blissful, languid weariness, as after lovemaking sometimes, with a man who is at ease with his own silence. Snow whirls through the air, real, soft snow, a Christmas snow, just as we remember it from our childhood, with presents done up in satin ribbons. Everyone around the table is smiling, Jean-Bernard, lovely Maria — even the contractor, who is always serious but for once forgets to calculate totals. His eyes glued to the window, he begins to talk about the great snowstorms of the past, which used to bring villages to a standstill, keep school-children cosily housebound. No one around the table has their minds on the cost of materials any more.

Jean-Bernard suggests we have a drink — we'll have the feeling we're playing hooky — we agree, the contractor too. Already the street lamps are coming on, and the city, immersed in snowflakes, looks just like a picture-postcard city, while the scotch splinters the ice cubes in our glasses. From here, you can't see the other city, the one without trees or birds, where poverty rules, where the windows are cracked, where the brick is grimy, the asphalt stained with urine and blood. It is absent from the window's darkening rectangle. We forget about it even when we bend over the plans of the school. All we think of is the word *economize*.

Reality is such a bore! How could that remark have slipped out of my mouth? Everyone stares at me in disbelief, even the contractor. Nobody has dared utter Jérôme's phrase since he left. We heard it hundreds of times, as soon as Jérôme got out his calculator and started to hum and haw before he'd eliminate a large stained-glass window, a light well, or a flight of marble stairs. How long will it be before that phrase, as trite as it may be, no longer makes us jump? How long does it take to forget? I look at my watch. In Rome, Alessandro is probably in bed by now. Who is he thinking of? Jasmina?

Jean-Bernard playfully waves his hand in front of my eyes. I must snap out of it and savour the snow again. I must try to pull myself together, as Mama used to say when I was small, do my best to come up with a funny face. But it's a waste of time, I just can't put on an act. I would like to let myself be covered by the soft and gentle Christmas snow. And stay there all winter long.

6

You've got mail. The rooster let out his silly cock-a-doodle-doo cackle, Alessandro's name appeared on the screen. I turned on the printer, I wasn't going to read his message right away, I would wait. Wait — wasn't that what I'd been doing for the past two days? Wait — as I never thought I still would, now that I have a liver spot on my hand? Did I mean so little to you, Alessandro? How could I tell? You meet someone among the ruins, and immediately there's the need to feel your heart pulsating with life within your chest, there's the sudden urge to love. You approach that person, you're foolish enough to fantasize about being taken, in a crumbling bedroom, right there, under the scorched sky. Then you go home. You forget. You start counting time again in weeks and months, until the next ruins, on your next trip.

I read. Greedily. I drank in the words until they were etched into my very soul. I read like a woman who has been expecting a letter from a man she already loves. As for Alessandro, he wasn't expecting anything, didn't dare hope for anything. *I'm almost an old man, Anna. Past the age of miracles. I walk alone, I'm moving towards an abyss I already know. But I would like to see you again, Anna, perhaps at Christmas-time, if you're free, if you're willing to welcome a man who has nothing to give.*

I turned off the light and stretched out on the sofa. I lay in a timeless, silent darkness, while my heart once again beat in unison with the world. The day faded away, the building site, too, along with the contractor's face. Soon I would be sound asleep. The phone rang, I heard my voice on the answering machine, then a man spoke — my father was at a nearby hotel, he was going back to Toronto the next day. I didn't pick up the receiver.

The lights of the city forced their way through the window, they drifted about overhead, they left Alessandro's soft shadow on the wall. Just like in those amateurish home movies that people project on their living-room walls on nights when they're bored. Who are you, Alessandro? I pictured the shy student whose steps echoed through the streets of Rome, on his way to the university, and then, later, carrying out his first excavations at Carthage. Sloping shoulders, a slight stoop, a kind of weariness that would always be with him. Or rather a gravity, yes, a gravity that had a cause, and a date: that summer evening when he was awakened by soldiers' voices in the kitchen. His mother's wailing. His father wouldn't be coming back. On that very day they'd celebrated his sixth birthday. Almost the age of reason. God's image suddenly faded away. From then on, churches would be desolate places, in spite of their smiling virgins and sprays of freshly cut flowers.

Sofia Moretti puts her coloured dresses away in the large wooden chest. She enters widowhood the way a woman enters a convent. From this day on, her children will only see her wearing black. Is your childhood real, Alessandro, or have I made it up, borrowed it from some novel? The well-behaved little boy that I see is sitting on the curb, he's watching the German soldiers on leave, impossibly tall and blond teenagers who don't even know how to say hello in Italian. In a few days' time they'll sail for Africa, they'll be hearing other, even stranger languages. Some day Alessandro will go to Africa, too. He swears this to Elsa, his little sister. He'll take her with him, he'll show her butterflies as large as birds, trees so tall they grow right through the heavens. For now, they play at being soldiers, the street becomes a battlefield, Alessandro strains to overhear a few German syllables from the blond teenagers. One evening, he'll greet his mother with the military salute, *Heil Hitler*. He'll receive his first smack, a smack that could have put his jaw out of joint. Later, he'll find out that his cousin has been arrested. They won't be seeing him again.

How about you? We will be seated at the table. I will have cooked a meal, salmon, perhaps, or veal. It will be my turn to fashion a childhood for myself. A pampered little girl, with a pampered little girl's heartaches. No brother or sister, no cousin who's under suspicion, no war. An uneventful story, with trivial occurrences. The pink bicycle, our tomcat chasing females every spring, needing to be nursed back to health by us after his fights, the seaside holidays with Anna. My aunt spends her days daydreaming on the beach, she points out ships in the distance to me, one day she'll set sail, she'll take a trip around the world, she'll make a stop in countries where there are princes. Yes, I'll tell you about Anna Martin — not everyone has an aunt who is mad. You'll ask, *Whose idea was it to call you Anne?* But by then you'll have poured yourself another glass of wine, you'll be listening to me with only half an ear. You will have come close to me, lifted my skirt, thrust your hand between my thighs. I don't want to imagine what happens next. We will invent it together.

7

I didn't take the time to turn up my coat collar, like a woman who has never experienced winter. Like Jasmina, perhaps, if she had come here. The city was shivering, so were the people on the street. They ran all the way to the subway entrances, expressionless faces hidden behind an air of resignation. It was only the first snowstorm. How many were there still to come? But a thin, watery light broke through the clouds, and people on the street looked up, they slowed down, they walked along almost quietly now, their cheeks getting used to being nipped by the cold again. Behind me, at the bus stop, two girls wondered if enough snow had fallen for them to get their skis out. I got on the crowded bus without paying attention to the reply. I was appeased, filled with happiness, that slightly anxious kind of happiness one sees in the faces of unbelievers. What if Alessandro couldn't make it? One of his sons might be ill, you never know, or there might be an accident, or another trip. Hadn't he mentioned he was going to take a group of students to Carthage? Anything might make him change his mind. Love is so fragile when the loved one is still only an image.

You've never been to my place, Alessandro, you don't know where I live. I haven't shown you photos of my university days, I haven't told you about my first love. You haven't seen the porcelain cats lined up on top of the bookcase in my bedroom, not even the one with the broken tail, you wouldn't be able to describe what I read before going to sleep. I have never undressed in front of you, Alessandro, you have never caressed the soft, smooth skin on my inner thighs. You have never explored the warm recesses of my body. You have never seen me cry.

Yes, I am anxious. You would make fun of me. You'll be here for Christmas, you said so. That engineer from Los Angeles had said the same thing, but he didn't come. Yet there had been letters, the phone ringing almost every night, the magic formulas of passion, and promises. I'd put flowers by the bed, I was at the airport an hour before his flight was due, I stood there, hoping, until all hope was lost.

Rue Sherbrooke. The driver booms it out. The bus stops, but only a couple of people manage to get off — we're squeezed together as tightly as pages in a book. We'll be late for work. The fun of the slight disruption spreads throughout the bus. People laugh, strike up conversations. A woman asks me if I was supposed to get off, too. I nod, yes I was, but never mind, I'll stay on till the subway. The woman winks at me — there's a sudden feeling of solidarity —then her voice is drowned out by the quiet rumble of the bus which has started moving again. And here are the gaping jaws of the subway, ready to swallow up the passengers.

A festive light washes over the city, an almost orangey glow. I feel like walking. I'll go and rummage about in bookstores, the ones where I might find something about the Phoenicians. I'll sit down in a small café and leaf through books. First, I'll look at the colour illustrations. Then the ones in black and white. After that, the captions below the pictures. Slowly, I'll move my finger over the words so I can touch them. I'll read the text at home, in bed, my legs wrapped up warmly in my duvet. When Alessandro arrives, I'll know everything there is to know about the Phoenicians. Because Alessandro will come. He will. We are going to defy destiny.

8

It looks like threads — black, bent threads — all of them the same length, around a tiny velvet button. The spider isn't moving right now but is lying stiffly in its web. It must be starving. No flies or butterflies, barely a few specks of dust. How will it survive until the spring? It waits without changing position, it doesn't appear to be bothered by the steam that rises from the bathtub. For three days now it has been in the left-hand corner, above the sink, where the wall meets the ceiling. I've tried to dislodge it with the broom, but it hurled itself into the air, then crashed down at my feet. Alive — dazed, but alive. I stared at it, feeling ashamed all of a sudden, as one should after a crime. I walked out of the bathroom. Yesterday morning it was just finishing repairing its web, it must have worked all night long. In the evening, it was back in its old spot. Since then, it's been on the look-out. I'm sure it will starve, but it needn't worry, I won't try to kill it again.

Today, for the first time, I was able to face Saturday without being afraid. I was going to bury myself in the only book I'd managed to hunt up about the Phoenicians, at the municipal library. In the bookstores, there was nothing. Studies on the Greeks, the Romans, the Egyptians. But nothing on Phoenicia. *An almost forgotten culture*, a bookseller told me, probably just

for something to say. I flinched. I was on the verge of men-
tioning Alessandro, but what would have been the use? After
tidying the apartment, I finally picked up the gorgeous hard-
back album. And then that barely audible scratching sound, a
rustling of wings, the call of a wounded bird. I cast a brief look
towards the front door before going back to sketches of ships
that used to ply unceasingly the waters of the Mediterranean.
But immediately there was a knock, distinct enough to make
me put my book down on the table. I got up. I opened the door.

A tall, slender form, muffled in old furs, was leaning
against the wall. She straightened up. She pulled off her tuque
and removed her seemingly endless scarf. I looked at her face,
framed by red hair, at the nose and the mouth, both covered
with rings. A small, subdued voice said, *Fanny*. I motioned to
her to come inside with barely concealed abruptness. What did
she want from me? Nevertheless, I took her heavy coat, which
was still icy to the touch, pointed to the sofa, offered her a cup
of coffee, and the young girl accepted with a smile. She pulled
a package of cigarettes from a jacket with as many holes in it
as there were in her lips. She asked me if it was all right to
smoke at my place. I went to the kitchenette to fetch the only
ashtray I still own and returned to sit down opposite her. Was
I annoyed or sympathetic? Perhaps just intrigued. Before I had
time to figure it out, I heard, *The woman who threw herself off
her balcony was my godmother.* That's when the afternoon shattered into countless images — jumbled, disconnected from one
another. Fanny's first real smile, the cigarette butts piling up in
the ashtray, the beer that followed the two cups of coffee, the
ham sandwich because she hadn't had a thing to eat yet, the

little notebook peeping out from the pocket of her jacket full
of holes, and the holes in her jeans, the holes in her stockings,
the holes in her skin, the holes in our conversation.

At some point, I don't know when, I walked over to the
window. The wind was dusting the balcony floor with fine dry
snowflakes — my eye fell on the bare branches in the pots.
Why had I let my dwarf roses die? In a kind of echo, I heard
Fanny's voice, *Did you see my aunt fall?* Reluctantly I nodded
yes. Fanny joined me. She stared into space, squinting into the
distance, as though her aunt's ghost might suddenly emerge
among the white shapes whipped up by the blowing snow.
Then, *My father says she was crazy.* Slowly, I looked down. The
darkening city was changing into a mass of dim, motionless,
shadowy forms, an abstract painting on a wall surrounding a
world now totally empty.

She's crazy, she's really crazy. That was my father's voice —
I used to overhear it through the half-open door of my bedroom when everyone thought I was asleep. What had Aunt
Anna done this time? Had she decided to go to the movies in
her dressing gown? Had she thrown water at a neighbour? Had
she informed on poor Monsieur Meunier because she thought
he was a Russian agent? The next morning, at the table, I
would find my father with his face buried in the newspaper,
he'd return my kiss without actually seeing me from behind his
horn-rimmed glasses, and I would slurp my cereal just so I'd get
his attention. If I was lucky, he'd say, *Anna, will you please eat
with your mouth closed?* I'd answer, *Anne. My name is Anne.*
Then Mama would add something in a falsely light-hearted
tone, and Papa smiled — he'd put his paper down on the

chequered tablecloth and spread his lips into a fake smile. He knew how to look happy even when he wasn't. He belonged to a theatrical company — sometimes he declaimed long mono-logues from *Cyrano*, accompanied by dramatic gestures. He made me take elocution lessons. One day, I was going to be a real actress, not an amateur like him. He really believed that.

Do you do any acting, Fanny? The tall, slender form next to me didn't respond. Then a faraway voice murmured, *No I don't, but I write poems. I'll bring you some of them next Saturday if you like.* I twitched, but heard myself reply, *Next Saturday's fine.*

9

Like gasping for breath, like choking, a sensation of being smothered that slowly fades away, and the air swells inside your chest again in long deep waves — you feel you're going to survive. Nowadays, I'm only able to explain things through images. Jean-Bernard nodded. He began a sentence, but the waitress came over to take our order. He would ask a few questions about the menu, he'd end up choosing his old standby *escalope aux fines herbes*, the waitress would leave again, and I would ask him what it was that he wanted to tell me. He'd squint at me as he answered, *I can't remember*, and the sentence would go and join the host of others that would never be spoken.

This time, however, he continued, *Yes, you feel you're going to survive*. The door opened and a group of young women walked in. They were laughing, having fun. They approached the Nativity scene set out beneath the artificial Christmas tree, and Jean-Bernard carried on, quipping, *To be truly alive, or to merely survive — that is the question*. He must have felt tired or bitter, he still missed Jérôme. No one at the office had really been able to take his place. I let slip, *None of us has his wild streak*, and I blushed, a little bit embarrassed. But Jean-Bernard agreed, *We're all too well-behaved*. He started to talk about

Jérôme, about their friendship, which had begun at classical college, about their university days, Jérôme's marriage. Besides, wasn't he the godfather of Jérôme's son, Étienne? Why had Jérôme left one morning, never to be heard from again? He wasn't an architect for nothing. He would tear everything down and then rebuild it somewhere else, on foreign soil. I said, *But we're not too badly off, though.* Jean-Bernard shrugged — we had talked about ourselves so many times. Our daring, our projects, all those contracts over the years. Our many loves. And our loneliness, not the peaceful solitude we enjoy at times of quiet reflection, but the loneliness of desolate Sundays, the minutes falling like drops of water from a dripping tap. Why weren't we in love with each other? Everything would have been so easy.

Jean-Bernard was now lifting pieces of the escalope to his mouth with a vacant look in his eyes — a tiny break in the regular order of things. He no longer heard the steady clattering of cutlery against dishes or the voice of Charles Aznavour, which was drowned out by the voices of the young women at the far end of the restaurant who were telling each other stories about the office. Had Jean-Bernard made love since his last boyfriend left? The young women were whispering now, they were sharing secrets, while Aznavour evoked the bohemian life of his younger years, that world of starving artists and women posing in the nude. I had a sudden vision of Fanny and I smiled. How old was she? Eighteen? Perhaps nineteen? I could have been her mother, and Jean-Bernard, with a little effort on his part, her grandfather. Alessandro, too. His eldest son, after all, wasn't much younger than I was.

You look pensive. Jean-Bernard had finished his plate, he focused on me again. Pensive? Yes, I was. All of a sudden an awareness of time took hold of my mind — time was no longer a collage of perfectly still moments, but rather a succession of bodies waltzing on the chessboard of the passing years. I covered Jean-Bernard's cold hand with my own. We would sit like this for a long, long while, to express a truth that reveals itself through gestures — I'm not in love with you, but I'm right here — insignificant gestures like bringing a cup of coffee, giving the gift of a book one has devoured the night before in bed, or a plant bought at the subway entrance, all those little gestures that we only appreciate once we realize how miserable life really is.

10

You haven't written *Cara mia* to me yet. Every time I get a message from you, I hope for it. Yet there's nothing, I'm not your Anna, Alessandro. Sometimes I'll dream up some kind of story about us. You are here, you are watching me breathe, in the pale morning light. You have put your wife's image in some recess of your memory, you are learning to love me. It's not just desire any more, but rather a hollow place inside your chest, a niche in which you would carry me around with you night and day. Even at the very moment when you'd discover the temple that was going to supply the key to all of Phoenician civilization. Even while leaving flowers on your wife's grave.

Today, I am stuck with your real story. It's my own fault, I had asked you to send me a photograph of you with your children, when they were small, and Jasmina. It's Jasmina I wanted to see, but I would never have admitted that to you. She was waiting for me this evening, concealed in the computer's darkness. All I had to do was press the print button, and she appeared next to you, smiling, happy. In love. Settled in a life I would never be part of. A spiteful tear formed at the rim of an eyelash — anger, of course, but also grief. Jealousy.

In the photo, Jasmina is very, very young. For the first time, I needed to face the obvious — you met Jasmina when she had just barely emerged from her teenage years. That's when you fell in love with her, her plump face, her perfect eyelids, her beautifully smooth, long, black hair. She doesn't look like the mother of the two little boys who are mischievously staring out at me — more like a big sister. You have wrapped your arm around her shoulder, you are protecting her. She is your enchanted forest, your festive music, your Jasmina.

One of the few photographs of our little family, that's what your message said. I don't believe you. There are more recent photos, taken in Rome at your son Marco's wedding, at your grandson's christening, or on a birthday. Or an afternoon in July, when your younger son has come from Florence, and click! someone presses the shutter — you will be together for all eternity. The small rectangle will gradually turn yellow on the sideboard shelf. Jasmina will stand before it, pick it up, look at it with a smile. That's the woman I would have liked to see, Alessandro, with circles under her eyes, her hair already dyed, and brown spots on her hands.

You want to humiliate me, Alessandro. Don't deny it. You're trying to show me that it's useless to struggle, that your life as a man is in the past, that all that is left for you now is the study of ruins. Or is it Jasmina's doing? Before dying, she may have torn up all the traces of time. I can see her, with a satisfied smile on her puffed-up face — she is watching herself burning in the dark flames, she is condemning you to the curse of her triumphant flesh, you will be hers forever. But I'm capable of stirring up the ashes. You don't know me. Years and years of studying to which everything needed to be sacrificed, scholarships so I could continue my education in Los Angeles, the training course in Paris,

the one in Berlin, two prizes already, and that television programme — my father called to congratulate me. Even his wife
insisted on speaking to me. *We're so proud of you, Ann.* I'm going
to fight, I swear to you I will, until Jasmina rots away beneath
the daisies in the cemetery at Rome or Carthage, I don't know
where you've buried her. I will not ask you.

For the past few minutes I've been trying to come up with
a silky phrase, which would steer you back to my black, lacy
underwear. A phrase that would highlight my own mysteries.
It's been no use wandering from the table to the sofa, from the
sofa to the bed — I've reread a hundred times the words now
smeared with mustard and makeup remover, the word *Thanks*,
for example, which was so hard to write, the word *wonderful*,
near it, in which I seem to hear my spiteful voice. *Thanks for
the wonderful photo.* I would like to add a few things to make
the adjective appear inoffensive. I don't want to set Jasmina
apart, but make her glorious breasts disappear beneath my
words, and not see your happiness, Alessandro. Divert the
attention to Marco's pout, stress how much he looks like you.
Isn't he your eldest, beloved son in whom you are well pleased,
as the Bible says?

Such a tight feeling in my chest as I click *Send.* Yet I need
to face the truth. Thirty-five years of life together, Jasmina's
body twice bearing your child, her beautiful breasts filled with
milk, then chapped — those little gluttons are fighting with you
for your sweetheart, but she returns to you every night, her body
heavier and heavier, more and more sedate. Thirty-five years,
twelve thousand seven hundred and seventy-five nights. How
many times have you found refuge in Jasmina's fragrant body?

My bedroom looks even darker now that the screen is blank. I should turn off the computer, go to bed, abandon the photograph to the stillness of the night. Or send you another message. Let's forget about everything, Alessandro. I'm not strong enough to struggle against Jasmina.

11

So what do you think of my poems? Fanny is right there, in front of me, with a worried expression in her eyes. She runs her hand through her red hair, she is waiting for a sign, a word, some gesture, looking like a little red bird whose feathers have got wet. She is watching my hand as it turns over the pages of her red notebook — a more vivid red even than her hair — while I am desperately searching for the right words. Then suddenly I approve, I like them, yes I do, this one in particular. A dimple forms in her full cheek, she starts to laugh, she puts her finger on the page. She says quietly, *I thought of you when I wrote that poem.* Laughter bubbles up in me, too. I blurt out, *Am I as sad as the woman in your poem, Fanny?* The face with the red halo turns serious again. Fanny shrugs, she will leave it at that.

I have to admit to her that I never read poetry. Works on architecture, yes, and the occasional novel, but never any poetry. I used to go to the theatre with my father, but now all I do is draw lines on plans, calculate angles, delineate spaces for windows, for doors, flights of stairs, or a light well, so that sunlight may stream into a room in December, on days like today, when the air is so mild that we dare to hope winter won't get the better of us. Architecture is also an art. Fanny sits cross-legged, withdrawing into a dreamy silence behind the smoke from her cigarette. I go into the kitchen to fetch more coffee. When she doesn't feel she is being observed, Fanny is already a woman. The curve of her shoulders, a certain elegance when she bends forward to stub out her cigarette in the ashtray, the way she peers into the sunbeams as they slant through the French doors. At the moment, I only know her first name.

She arrived without warning, picked up the ashtray, settled down on the sofa in front of me and just sat there for a long while without saying a word. She finally surfaced from her day-dream with the question, *Are you feeling better today?* Instantly I answered, *Yes,* the way we close our eyes at the movies at the beginning of a scene we can't bear to watch. *Yes, I am,* I repeated, and I changed the subject, I talked about the upcoming holidays, did she have any plans? *You are lying,* she replied. But are you really lying when you try to cope with a wall that gets higher and higher and higher every day? Sometimes all it takes is a smile, or a tight-fitting dress you feel like buying. You pay with your card, you are going to attract attention at the reception at city hall, a gorgeous engineer will offer to take you home, you'll pretend you don't notice his wedding-band, you will script your role as you go along, and while the evening lasts, you believe in it.

Aren't you saying anything? Fanny sounds a little shrill, she would like an answer and, for some strange reason, I go and get the photograph. I keep repeating to myself, you are crazy, she is eighteen years old, but nevertheless I tell her — Alessandro, Jasmina, Jasmina, Alessandro. Fanny listens, staring down at the floor. Then she takes the photo in her chubby hands and watches the figures one by one as they detach themselves from the group, Alessandro, Jasmina, Marco, and tiny Gianni on his mother's lap. Finally, she leaves the photo on the table with a sigh. *You are being so stupid, so unbelievably stupid.* Now I pick up the photograph. I study it until the faces become a tangle of dead, meaningless lines that have no power over the present. Fanny hands me her cigarette lighter. Unthinking, I go over to the fireplace, I light the lighter. In just a few seconds, there is nothing left. Except ashes.

Get your coat. We're going out. A sparkling haze hangs over the city, with strings of Christmas lights, and Nativity scenes that show the same child year after year. I take Fanny's arm. The two of us make a funny pair, red hair and black hair almost touching, with the sleeve of my mohair coat disappearing into the moth-eaten fur. We stroll along, we watch the reindeer in the store windows, and Santa Clauses dragging heavy bags stuffed with empty packages. Fanny is happy. She stops, points out the window decorations. Slowly, I'm beginning to see Alessandro as the man I knew in Carthage, I'm beginning to wait for him again. Yes, in the desolate darkness of my body, I am waiting for him.

Part II

1

I simply can't picture his gestures, match them with the gestures of men when they undress a woman. The buttons of the blouse, the skirt, the carefully chosen underwear which will end up on the carpet — a little heap of rags. Since I heard his voice on the telephone, I've been unable to picture him. *Hello Anna.* Those words were enough to blur his image, they entered my pores and anchored themselves in an old fear. He must have detected the trembling in my voice when I said, *I'm waiting for you.* He must have, because he murmured, *I'm afraid, Anna.* I didn't respond. There was a long silence, magnifying the noises from the Fiumicino airport, and in the middle of that silence the black underthings laid out on the bed suddenly struck me as ridiculous. Pathetic. I had to make an effort to concentrate so I could say, *See you in a few hours, Alessandro,* before he hung up. I put everything away, just as though I'd been caught in the act. The underwear, the bottle of champagne, even the flowers in the bedroom. This time I would play my role without any props.

The ordeal of the body. I'm afraid just like you, Alessandro. Every first time. An old, hidden, visceral terror. Dread, every time, before a feat that is too great for us humans. *You will be one flesh.* We must deaden our fear. We invent scenarios, create a body for ourselves that hides our real body, and a skin we believe to be suited to love, we search for jewellery, for garters, we emphasize the contour of our breasts, we put on makeup, we try to take our mind off things. Then we are reassured. We feel free, optimistic, we accept the beginning without thinking about the end, we don't see our body as that of a big bird folding back its wings as it falls. We don't see we are falling, spinning down into a bottomless abyss.

You are flying at the moment, Alessandro. You are defying the sea as it bristles with spiky peaks. It rages, it threatens, but you won't let it swallow you up. You will come to me, in all your nakedness. I will warm you, caress you, my body will quietly cover you. Love. Perhaps we need to believe before we can fall in love. A believer — that's how I see you, Alessandro, kneeling down in the soil at Carthage, red fingernails reaching into the red earth with the necessary gentleness in every movement, with the faith one needs to continue when the soil yields nothing. And waves of discouragement, a desire to relinquish the past to its mysteries, the impulse just to give up. One simply stops trying to spin the web between cause and effect.

Perhaps you will like my spider, still hanging up there in the corner of the bathroom. It's a survivor. Like Fanny, who writes her poems every day. And like me, Alessandro. I am numb with fear, but I am going to love you. Despite the terror that clings to my crazy first name, I *am* going to love you.

2

The airplane looms up in the distance as though it were emerging from the countryside, dragging its heavy body through rose-coloured cotton wool. The snow has almost obliterated the runway, and all around everything is uniformly white. This is Alessandro's first image, a long strip of white, frozen, barren earth. Which has no smell, no fragrance. Does he already miss Rome as he sits there wedged in his seat? Is he wondering why he decided to come and spend the holidays with a woman whose voice he barely knows? Perhaps he is already counting the days that separate him from his life back home, a life that doesn't belong to me.

I am counting, too. About fifteen minutes to disembark, then customs and the luggage. In less than an hour we'll find ourselves face to face, intimidated, awkward. There will be the usual platitudes, *Did you have a nice trip?* We will work very hard at getting rid of the silence.

I keep looking up at the big clock, which won't let people forget the time. I'm trying to be patient, as when Mama used to make me come with her to the railroad station. Papa was returning from Toronto, I had to abandon the building I was assembling out of tiny red bricks. I would wash my face, then dive into the Meteor, deliberately slamming the door. But

Mama wouldn't hear. She was holding the steering wheel in a funny way, because of the smart-looking nail polish that wasn't quite dry yet. She would check her makeup in the rear-view mirror, she was humming to herself. At dessert time, Papa would yawn, he'd want to go to bed early. Mama always agreed, and it was useless for me to ask if I could watch the movie on television. I put on my good-little-girl mask — they'd start paying attention to me again the next morning.

Now there's a commotion. The arrival door slides open and then closes again, a monstrous mouth spitting out travellers. A woman with her pink poodle, a couple of newly-weds, a few business men, and old people dressed in black, so bent over that it's amazing they're able to push their carts filled with boxes. People are jostling each other, they're shouting, weeping, kissing. This is the Italy of post-war movies, the one of bicycle thieves and poverty, Alessandro's homeland when he was chasing sixteen-year-old girls. There he is, a little stooped, tired-looking. He stops, squints into the harsh light. He is searching for me, and I push my way through the crowd, I run towards him, throw myself into his arms. What kind of a couple do we make, I wonder, with my black ringlets tangled up in his white curls?

Everything is grey now — the trees, the road, the sky, even the snowflakes that land softly on the taxi's windshield, and the highways meeting up with other highways in a vast network, a maze. Then the city, the neon lights, the streets swarming with people at rush hour, the traffic jams. The taxi driver sighs, blurts out a few words in Arabic. Alessandro lets go of my hand and answers him in Arabic, he becomes animated, he is suddenly in

Carthage. All I understand is the names of cities, Tunis, Sousse, which ring out like the names of women, conjuring up Jasmina's glorious face. I close my eyes, I pray for some apparition that might save me. I see Fanny's form. She hands me her cigarette lighter. I light it. I am trying to light Jasmina's funeral pyre, but perhaps the fire will consume me, too.

3

Circles, spirals, curls. Alessandro is drawing with his fingertips in the down of my arms, as if he were slowly trying to accept love's will. He doesn't dare touch the delicate skin of my neck yet, or slide his palm over to my moist breasts. I am holding my breath, I am afraid to move. He hasn't caressed another woman's body since Jasmina died. I know, now I know. And before, when Jasmina was alive? I'll never ask. The room is getting chilly, the logs have burned themselves out, we should rekindle the flames. Never mind. I must lie totally still, leave everything as it is, wait for desire to win out over death.

Such silence around us, such a tranquil, meditative silence. Alessandro slips his hand underneath my sweater. Then a feathery touch, and we are in the darkness of love, already joined in one solitude. That diamond between Alessandro's eyelashes — what words are haunting him right now? His weeping mother pledging fidelity to his father, or Jasmina imploring him never to forget her? I move my lips towards him, run them lightly over the soft skin just below his eye, over his beard and then, hesitantly, over his lips, as if it were a first confession. My *love*. The phrase formed too quickly in my mouth, the phrase of a woman who has no one to mourn. Did Alessandro hear? His lips feel almost hard on mine, then his tongue enters my mouth, he licks me, he wants to swallow all my words. He yields now, I can tell, his whole body, the blood in his veins, despite memory, Jasmina's magnificent hair, their quarrels, their fits of helpless laughter, the soft light in their Tunis house, the rapture in the afternoon while the boys were having their nap, the splendour of the flesh once again fulfilling the promise of love.

I love you, Alessandro, I say, swept up in a whirlwind nothing can stop any more. Between us, there's now only us, trembling, alive — us, and the infinite arrogance of oblivion. I love you. It isn't a confession, but rather a way of bringing him to me, while he thrusts his blood-filled flesh into my body, a sweet violent heat, an explosive burst as if all our fibres were flying into space, a great whirling of cells, a golden dust, a return to the calming, impenetrable, unfathomable depths before the separation of land and waters. We are no longer anyone.

Alessandro cradles my head in his hands and looks at me, slowly, as if trying to get used to the ordeal of my face. He stares at me, dazed, sad, guilty. Jasmina has just gone back to her ashes, he hasn't been able to keep her eternally alive in death. I wish I could think of something to say, to comfort him, redeem him, but my silence merges with the silence of the night. A deep shiver runs up my spine. This is the present again, the body craving a little warmth, crying out louder than all my worries. I shiver and Alessandro recognizes my face. He smiles at me, presses me against him, wraps me in his jacket. A lover's gesture, or that of a friend, or a widower? I can't tell, I never can when compassion is involved. And I don't really want to know.

4

He's asleep. Tightly pressed against my skin, he's asleep, over-come by weariness. His breathing on the nape of my neck sounds a little raspy. It isn't a snore, but something like a whistle, a moaning, the sound of a musical instrument that is out of tune, or a clumsy caress. I will watch over him until darkness enfolds us. The lights from the city are tracing ghosts on the curtains, but they don't threaten us. Alessandro lies, untroubled, against my warm back. In the truthfulness of sleep, he has separated my body from Jasmina's. I am not afraid.

Alessandro slides a little bit away from me now, he makes sudden movements, he is struggling. I gently stroke his arm and he clings to me again. He reaches for my fur. He mumbles, *Anna*, he recognizes me and quietens down. There, he is quiet again. No, I don't need to be afraid. Our bodies are already fused together in an age-old story we will never comprehend. *People don't lie when they're asleep.* How often did Mama say that? But I never paid any attention, I was too preoccupied. Life was taking up all the space — my studies, work, my lovers, fellow students of architecture. And then there was that hand-some American I met at the bar where I worked, near the Citadel. Mama occasionally came for a drink there after Papa had gone off to live with Eileen in Toronto. I sometimes wonder if Papa would have kept up the happy-little-family act if the stage hadn't collapsed right in front of our eyes, in the middle of the performance.

When I told Alessandro, he looked stunned. He drained his glass in one gulp, staring into space and saying over and over, *Just like a soap opera.* An innocent question had started it off. *How about your father, Anna?* I'd forgotten the shame, I told him the story. How Papa's firm had merged with a company in Toronto, Papa's trips, how he stayed in Toronto more and more frequently, then his job over there, his need for new challenges, he was only forty-five after all. Mama had her job as a trained nurse, and she looked after Anna so well you would've thought she was her own sister rather than Papa's! I was at university. When he did come home, we always had fun, Mama would wear dresses that fitted tightly around her hips and take us out to a different restaurant every time. I remember it all perfectly, we were sitting at a table, about to have our meal. Papa asked me a question about my studies. I answered him with a last trace of my childhood days still lingering in my voice — all those walks by the river to watch ships from fabled lands, and the inevitable chocolate-dipped ice cream cone. Yes, I remember. Then that man coming out of nowhere while the waiter was bringing us our plates. He didn't seem to notice us, he only saw Papa, whom he called Richard, in English. He talked very, very fast, he was in town for a convention, he was going back to Toronto the following day. And when was Papa going back? Hadn't Eileen come along? Had she stayed at home with her little Michael? What a delightful little boy she had! I heard a faint *Yes.* A stranger with an anglophone name, Richard Martin, the lover, perhaps even the life partner, of someone called Eileen, had just taken my father's place at the table.

Alessandro now moves his hand towards my breasts. Mama knew about Eileen, she knew all along without really knowing. One simply knows these things, she says. One might try to blame it on fatigue, or the long train rides, or problems at the office, but when people are asleep they don't lie. She knew, but she pretended not to notice. Just as I know about Alessandro. I don't need to be afraid.

5

Freshly ground coffee, tobacco burning in the bowl of a pipe, a maple log, Alessandro's sleep smell in the sheets — I open my eyes in a lived-in space. This year I'll spend Christmas Day in a lived-in space. What time is it? How long has Alessandro been up? Questions hanging in the air. Drowsily I let them hover there, I'm still clinging to a dream that has left me feeling happy, as if it were possible to step out into empty space without any risk of me shattering my bones. That would make a good beginning for a poem, Fanny would say. She would pull her red notebook out of her pocket.

She's off to join her new boyfriend in the country today, she'll be meeting his family — mother and father living together, brothers and sisters, a dog. Pure bliss. I smiled without making any comment. Alessandro and I are going to spend Christmas Eve alone together. I've patiently planned our meal, I so enjoy doing simple things. Washing mushrooms for the salad, wiping away a tear that's about to fall on the freshly chopped onions, then calculating not the dimensions of a building, but the cooking time for the goose or when I should bring out the entrée.

Leaning out over the city, Alessandro lazily chews on his pipe. He is trying to identify the vertical masses in the snowy morning light. A church, recognizable by its steeple, buildings, high-rises in the distance, the silos at the harbour. I quietly go up to him and gently touch his arm. He turns around, *Did you sleep well, Anna?* He pushes an unruly lock of hair that's covering my right eye back behind my ear. *I've just made you some of that dishwater you call coffee.* I stick out my tongue at him, he laughs. The night hasn't driven us apart.

The flames shoot up, tall, bold, triumphant. Then the log disintegrates. With a smile, Alessandro turns to face me. *I feel at home here.* I take his hand in mine, I try to picture his life in Rome, his apartment amid the screeching street noises of Rome. I'm going to ask him to draw it for me, when I have the strength. Right now, our story fits in the cup of our hand — one afternoon at Carthage, an evening in Tunis, the remembrance of three nights in my bed. Nevertheless, there are memories. The endless waiting in December, the messages, the doubts. Jasmina's photograph. And, luckily, Fanny, my red-haired angel, who appeared just at the right time, as in the days when angels would come down from heaven to save us. *Alessandro, were there any angels in Carthage?* He gives me an amused look. He buries his hand into the opening of my dressing gown. He isn't going to answer.

6

The darkness slowly advanced and we let it spread until everything was swallowed up — the chairs, the lamps, the Christmas tree, even the window and the pinkish-black, velvety sky. I tried to get up to put a disc in the CD player, but Alessandro placed his hand on my arm, why deprive ourselves of the silence and, at the very heart of this silence, the life of the building which reached us in slow waves? Just then, the laughter of a Santa Claus rang out in the corridor, young children gave little shouts of joy, and we started to laugh, feeling joyful as well, captives of a dim past that was stirring in us again as if it had simply been dozing for a while. Alessandro got up, groped his way to the bedroom, came back with a present, put it under the Christmas tree. Then I took an art book, which Fanny had helped me wrap, out of the cupboard. And also my present for her, an anthology of poems recommended by the bookseller. Too bad I wouldn't be able to give it to her this evening. Now I would miss hearing her clap her hands, her whoop of delight. Until what age, I wonder, do the joys of childhood call for noise, for chuckling, for a bit of a racket, which reassures us we're capable of being loved?

Alessandro wanted to talk to his grandson. I heard his voice in Italian, a lilting, sonorous voice all of a sudden. He wasn't quite the same man any more, as when we go back to our first language. Younger, more playful, his Christmas voice, without the slightest trace of nostalgia. He abruptly stopped talking, placed his hand over the receiver and said, *Anna, Marco would like to say hello to you.* Taken aback, I answered, *I don't speak Italian,* but then I thought, wasn't Jasmina Tunisian? Marco must have learned French at the same time as Arabic and Italian.

I stood facing the city now ready to welcome the crucified child, and talked to Marco from the photograph, the mischievous little boy I had reduced to ashes with Fanny's help. I heard myself wishing him a merry Christmas. When I hung up, my eyes met Alessandro's. His son had just given him the Christmas present he'd been hoping for — he had drawn a line between the past and the present. A porous line, but it was nevertheless a stroke, a boundary. I said, *Your son is very nice.* Little drops trickled down into Alessandro's beard. He added, *It won't be as easy with Gianni.* The photograph rose once again from its ashes and, a little bit to the right, a chubby baby, curled up in the warmth of Jasmina's body. Why had I burned that photo? I would have liked to see it again, to study Gianni's posture, the expression on his face, to focus on the details I had missed. I had barely even looked at the children, and now they were becoming real, they were turning into men who might say yes or no, men who were very much alive, who could no longer be tucked away in a souvenir album.

My head was spinning again. The woman's dress, open like a parachute, her fixed lips, her eyes smiling at me for a brief moment. I heard a sniff beside me, the sound of someone quietly weeping, I, who had never seen a man cry. Alessandro was sobbing. He looked older, shrunken. Haggard. I silently put my arms around him, as his mother and Jasmina must have done, his sister too, perhaps, and other women whom I would never know by name — women friends, lovers for one evening or for a month or two, who would have crossed his path at Carthage, at that time of day when the blazing sun forces people inside. Suddenly, I was a different woman. Who was I now? It didn't matter. Alessandro was sobbing, he needed to be consoled, I comforted him. On the wall, a gigantic two-headed creature had formed. It slowly swayed in its own shadow. Perhaps I wasn't a woman any more, perhaps Alessandro and I were no longer human beings, but monsters, flying fish, or crabs that together were trying to burrow into the earth's crust. Between us, there was only us, with our fragile story. We weren't safe anywhere.

7

You look like my grandfather. Alessandro put his fork down on his
plate and burst out laughing — a loud, hearty, pealing laugh,
like a coughing fit. Fanny looked down and said, *My grandfather
is a handsome man.* Wiping his eyes, Alessandro patted her hand
to show her he understood, then his shoulders started to shake
again, he dissolved into laughter all over again. To reassure her
I said, *You know, we don't realize how time flies.*

Only an hour before, I'd gone down to the store in my
building with Fanny, and I had jumped when a man said,
Mother and daughter. What a charming sight. Fanny had slipped
her arm through mine and beamed a radiant smile at the man,
while I made a feeble attempt at spreading my lips. In the elevator she'd said, *Isn't it great that people take you for my mother?*
I felt like shouting out, *No, Fanny, I don't want to be taken for
your mother.* But again I produced a polite smile.

The osso bucco on my plate is already lukewarm, all it took
was a few minutes. I'm studying the brown spot on my left
hand, a half-closed eye that is watching me. At first, you think
it's a bruise, you must have knocked against a doorpost, but the
eye doesn't vanish, it keeps on observing you. One day you
know it's there to stay, and you reflect on your mother's hands,
looking more and more like your grandmother's hands, with

their thick, purple veins, which seemed like a witch's hands to you when you were a child.

Mama sounded optimistic when she phoned yesterday to wish me happy holidays. The sun, the sea, the hotel — she described everything. *And your Aunt Anna is in excellent health*, she said, articulating every syllable so I would understand. I understood. No tantrums about trivial things, no reproaches, the South was still doing her a world of good, the voices in her head had faded. For the moment. They would reappear when the plane touched down on the frozen asphalt. I asked Mama to transmit my good wishes to Anna. I heard my aunt call out *Merry Christmas* from the far end of the room. That was a good sign, it really was — for how many years now had she not spoken to me? One day, when I opened the cupboard at Mama's place, I spotted a box done up with a ribbon which I had left for Anna. She had refused my present. Mama shrugged it off as usual, why puzzle over it? She had got used to Anna's mood swings, the way one gets used to sudden changes in temperature in winter, when blustery winds rage overhead and all we can do is wait for more tranquil skies.

Alessandro had wanted to know all about Anna. I told him what I knew, not a lot actually — it was a kind of madness for which there was no explanation, an ordinary kind of madness, the one they never show in television reports. I had gone to fetch photographs. I showed him the tiny yellowed rectangles, Anna and Papa with their parents, Anna at her first communion, Anna as a teenager, and Anna transformed into an elegant young woman. *You look like your aunt.* I knew that, I'd been told so many times. I was quite happy to look like that woman, but not the other one, the one I had known, the fat woman who'd undergone electroshock treatments and who'd had to take all those drugs. Anna had been beautiful until she was twenty-two, Papa used to say. But then there had been that war inside her head, good people and wicked people. Her brain had been bombed like a city, it couldn't be rebuilt any more. In my bed at night, when I was a little girl, I used to try to chase away all the soldiers who might have sneaked up on me.

Alessandro laughed at that. He has never been afraid of madness. He asked me, *Haven't you ever felt the urge to write?* I shrugged. I need lines and equations, rooms neatly aligned along corridors, I need concrete walls. Writing is Fanny's mad passion. Now she's the one Alessandro is making fun of. *Don't pull a face like that — obviously I look like a grandfather.* I shiver. Soon he'll be sixty-two years old, what is ahead for him? The same thing that awaits us all, even Fanny, and I'm in no mood for laughing. But I hear Alessandro say to Fanny, *Do you think we'll get Anne to laugh?* He doesn't call me Anna any more.

8

The north wind was gusting furiously at that time of day when the bleached sun might be mistaken for the moon. A fierce gale. Everything began to bend, trees, awnings, the people on the street. Even hotel flags curled around their poles. For a few hours there would be no more countries, no borders, only a besieged territory, from the north to the south, from Gaspé to New York. Alessandro settled himself in front of the window with my binoculars. Mesmerized, he called out to me every couple of minutes, he would want to show me something I had seen hundreds of times — a seagull huddled up in a recess of a cornice, someone's hat blown off by the wind, the nude girl on a neon sign, swaying her hips while waiting for clients. Alessandro's laughter rang out again and again, he laughed just as spontaneously as he sometimes might burst into tears, or get angry.

Suddenly he pointed his finger in the direction of the Vieux-Port. He said something in Arabic. He was speaking to Jasmina. She could loom up at the most unexpected times, and my heart would begin to race. Even in my dreams. The previous night I'd woken up with a start. She was hiding in the bedroom, a dark ghost straight out of a Bergman film. It was definitely her, I recognized her thick hair. Alessandro was asleep. I had clung to him for a bit of warmth but hadn't been able to go back to sleep. I'd kept my eyes fastened on the flickering patch of light on the wall — daybreak was bound to drive Jasmina away. The morning had finally come. Alessandro woke up feeling fresh and energetic. I suggested a long walk in the city, I would take him to places Jasmina had never known. And now the north wind suddenly brought her back to life. No battle was ever really won. Alessandro repeated his sentence in Arabic, then realized what he was doing. With the binoculars still in his hand, he came towards me.

I couldn't hold back my tears, big oily tears that left tiny spots on my blouse. If only Fanny had been here. She would have taken out her cigarette lighter, she would have burned this moment. Alessandro would again point his finger at the Vieux-Port, blurt out his remark in Arabic once again, and I'd go up to him with a forced smile, I'd even manage to laugh along with him. My high spirits would chase Jasmina away. Now, each one of my tears was making her grow a little bit more important. She should thank me, I was the one keeping her alive. I ought to learn from Eileen.

That dark shadow in Eileen's eyes when, many moons ago, I'd reminded Papa of a long-ago vacation by the sea. Papa hadn't said anything. He'd gloomily taken the last sip of his wine. He must have had a sudden vision of Mama's tanned body which he covered with sun lotion every morning, her rounded breasts. Does one ever completely forget? Eileen had been able to repress her tears behind a charming smile. With a twinkle in her eye she'd asked for the bill. How about going for a liqueur at that student bar I'd mentioned to them? Papa had snapped out of his daydream. Thanks to his dear Eileen he would fall asleep that night with a lovely image — he wasn't such a bad father after all.

We don't know why one day our tears finally stop flowing. More because of weariness, no doubt, than an easing of our pain. Or because in the end our heart simply dries up, like a desert stream. Then we accept the life already lived, and old stories. They lived happily ever after and had lots of children. But in our story the children would never be mine. They would always belong to Jasmina.

9

Mama's postcard arrived this morning, displaying the usual postcard scenery — a motionless sea, palm trees, the beach, parasols and, of course, the sun, an all-consuming sun, ringed with a garish yellow light. I glanced at the three or four pen-scribbled sentences. I knew already I would be reading the words of a woman who'd relinquished her own voice until the end of the vacation. A woman who was neither happy nor unhappy, as when we've lost our memory, when our mind is a blank. Then I read. About the summery weather, the hotel which was a marvel, the food, my aunt getting back her colour. With every trip, I saw those same words, always the warm weather, the hotel, the food, and Anna. I reread them while running my fingers over the tiny, round, intertwined loops, as I tried to uncover some hidden truth, something just for me that I might have missed. But of course there was nothing, there were no words underneath the words. Silently, I handed the card to Alessandro. He squinted at Mama's small handwriting. He said, *I've kept all my mother's letters.* The Pompeii letters, from the time of the first excavations, the Tunesian ones. Those that had been found in his father's pocket after he was killed in action. Simple letters about life, the children — Elsa had had chickenpox, and he, Alessandro, kept on growing and growing, in spite of all the hardships. This was the unspectacular side of the war, the one without the medals. I tried to picture a woman my age, tall and strong and dignified, making her way through the streets of Rome, holding her children by the hand. That woman didn't suffer any dizzy spells, or fits of despair.

The telephone rang. Jean-Bernard had just got back, he'd had a marvellous vacation, he was going to throw a New Year's Eve party for all his old friends. He added with a laugh, *And for a charming young man.* Would I come? I grimaced. I didn't feel like introducing Alessandro to my colleagues from work. I was being superstitious, but not completely. Had any of my love affairs ever lasted? The humiliation when you have to say, *It's over.* And the compassion, which is harder to bear than anything else. Jean-Bernard knew all this, of course, but he tried to persuade me, we could drop in very briefly, Alessandro and I. I was just going to refuse when my eyes met Alessandro's behind a curtain of smoke. He was following the conversation, and I gave in.

I hung up the receiver a little bit too abruptly. Alessandro jumped. I tried to explain things to him — from now on there wouldn't be that safe place deep inside me any more, where my hopes and my dreams might quietly gather. He didn't understand. What a pleasure to meet the people I went to lectures with in the evening after work. Weren't my colleagues part of my life? That was just it. A cold shiver ran down my spine, as when you feel threatened. Perhaps Alessandro was going to discover my other smile, the one that resembled the smile of the woman falling into empty space.

I had actually tried to question Fanny but didn't find out very much. Only some details, which one could count on the fingers of one hand. Her godmother had been a strange woman. Lately, she'd stopped spoiling her goddaughter, she would stare out at the world through a dirty window. Fanny's father had never been able to stand her. What else? Fanny had shrugged her shoulders, she would ask her mother. But she'd forgotten. I hadn't queried her again. I hadn't thought about it any more. Christmas was approaching, I needed to get ready for Alessandro's visit. There was also that new building site, and Jasmina's smile, which had gradually replaced the smile of the woman falling through empty space.

The woman falling through empty space. Ever since Alessandro arrived, I'd almost forgotten about her. Oddly enough, he was the one who steered me back to her. The two of us were walking along. He suddenly stopped and pointed to a huge smile suspended in the blazing blue sky above the museum. I gripped his arm. I instantly had a vision of the woman's lips, but he bubbled with enthusiasm — that woman up there had my lips. He wanted to know everything, the artist's name, what the painting was called. We might be able to buy reproductions. Without saying a word, I let myself be pulled along to the museum's entrance. Fortunately, the museum was closed for renovations. By the time it re-opened its doors, Alessandro would be strolling quietly through the streets of Rome. I began to breathe again. I wouldn't need to tell him the truth, the whole truth. But some day I would have to. Unless I could learn how to make my way, tall and strong and dignified like his mother, through the streets of Montreal. Or Rome.

10

It was there, all huddled up in its web, motionless, as if it were caught in its own trap. I watched it for a moment without the slightest twinge of sadness. Death had become an abstract fact again, a jumble of lines and angles, one of those unreadable blueprints on which you just can't picture a real house. Beneath the soap bubbles my hand looked perfectly smooth, the liver spot had vanished. I sank deep into the scalding-hot water and listened. A female voice drifted towards me, one of those Italian voices that can shatter the world and splinter the soul. In just a few hours the year would be ending, with its gallery of faces. The old ones, and those that had been added this past year. Alessandro, Fanny, the woman falling through space. So far, I'd been able to make two separate lists, but just as the old year slipped away, Alessandro would be wishing Jean-Bernard a happy New Year. And lovely Maria, my favourite colleague, would be offering her good wishes to Fanny.

Actually, Fanny's smoker's voice now drowned out that of the opera singer. She had just arrived and was talking to Alessandro. Try as I might to overhear what they said, I only managed to catch a few isolated sentences, and echoes of anger, the predictable phrases one always hears in conversations after a love affair has ended. Those phrases that I myself had uttered, too, filling them with rage, sometimes hatred, and anguish. Great suffering always brings out our spitefulness. I sank back even deeper under the bubbles, relieved to discover I had a human soul similar in every respect to other human souls. Now Alessandro spoke. I could hear a hint of amusement in his voice. He was trying to console Fanny, she would meet another boy some day, she was going to be happy. I made an effort to picture her fifteen years from now, without her red hair. Without her provocative image. Her theatrical appearance. What kind of look would there be on Jean-Bernard's face when he saw her later this evening?

One hour earlier, we'd had a phone call. A flood of words mixed with sobs had poured from the receiver — things had taken a tragic turn. Fanny had just found out that her boyfriend was going to spend the evening in his village with a female friend. He didn't know if he loved her any more. Her aunt's smile flashed through my mind. I ordered her to come over, to come over right away, I was waiting for her. Alessandro had closed up his book again. He was looking at me with a smile. He must have been reliving some long-ago heartbreak, the aimless wanderings through a Rome suddenly bloodless, no longer breathing, stripped of its cats, its street merchants, its quarrels, its declarations of love and war under crucifixes in cafés, under porticoes of movie houses and churches. A city that had come to a halt. He said playfully, *Her name was Amalia.*

Now Fanny laughed through her tears, while I dried my hair. Alessandro had a gift for giving a comical twist to even the tiniest detail — a passionate sigh, a glance, a touch. Then the dizzying plunge into despair when one is abandoned.

Fanny kept the conversation going, she asked all kinds of indiscreet questions, and Alessandro told stories, explained things, sorted out sentiments and emotions. Until he confessed, *Then Jasmina came into my life.* Fanny stubbed out her cigarette without asking anything this time. And Alessandro didn't elaborate.

Electric music suddenly filled the room. Guitars, drums, and a synthesizer waged war against the singer — a new group Fanny wanted us to hear. As she stood by the hi-fi system, facing the beautiful and barbarous city, every limb of hers quivered. Was this a dance or an exorcism? She noticed we were watching her and she cried out, *Come and dance with me!* I shook my head, but Alessandro got up. Stunned, I saw him walk towards Fanny, I saw him make a first attempt at swaying his hips, then a second one. He started to move his hands and his feet. He imitated Fanny. He was undulating before the city's neon lights. The present had won, this was a joyful celebration of the present moment. Alessandro pulled my arm. I had to get up. I imitated the two of them — the way they moved their heads, their upper bodies, their legs. Fanny was laughing, so was Alessandro. I began to laugh, too. In just a few hours we would all be wishing each other love and happiness. We would merrily plunge into the new year.

11

All of the present was contained in a single image. On the left, Maria, Marc, and Dominique were setting out salads on the table. On the right, Fanny listened with an intent frown, so as not to miss anything. Étienne, the son of Jérôme Langlois, was telling her something which the cacophony immediately swallowed up. In the middle stood Alessandro and Jean-Bernard, uncorking champagne. *Only three minutes to go before midnight*, an old friend of Jean-Bernard shouted out. He began the countdown. Instantly, my lovely image was swept away by a tidal wave surging through the dining room. Alessandro turned around to see where I was. I managed to slip through the crowd up to him, dodging people's elbows, and I cradled his face in my hands at the very moment when a voice amplified by all the other voices shouted out, *Happy New Year!* Alessandro held me close, I was beginning the year snuggled up in his smell. I had a feeling I was going to end it that way, too. I heard myself say, *It's going to be a wonderful year, you'll see.* Alessandro replied, *But I know it will.*

He would be leaving in a few days. I would have to relearn the rituals of being alone. Meals shared with a book, sleeping in a bed that seemed too big, trying to find things to do on Saturday, exchanging words of love by e-mail. Having Fanny take me off to a café near the college. When would Alessandro and I get together again? There were no definite plans whatsoever. Alessandro let the days drift by just as though we never needed to part. Yet a date should be set, and a place — Carthage or Rome. But it was probably too soon for the apartment in Rome. Would I be able to undress in Jasmina's bedroom?

Now Fanny approached with a glass in her hand and with laughing, brightened eyes. *When one is eighteen …*, Alessandro whispered in my ear. She pulled Étienne along with her. He was beginning to look more and more like Jérôme — his build, the dimple in his chin. I had to force myself not to ask him if he'd heard from his father. What woman was Jérôme with now? Fanny proudly introduced Alessandro to Étienne, alluding to Africa, Phoenician tombs, hinting at a life of adventure. Alessandro entered into the spirit of the game. He gesticulated, he told anecdotes I hadn't heard before. How much did I really know about him? Just a few memories that had slipped out during some conversation — children splashing about in the Fountain of Trevi, Rome being trampled under fascist soldiers' boots. But it's Alessandro who suddenly emerged, the little boy I hadn't known, the rebellious teenager, the diligent student, the man who was deeply loved. For he had been passionately loved — it always shows in men.

Another wave, a small one this time. More people were arriving, other guests coming by to offer their best wishes. Shouts, roars of laughter. Then the delicate touch of shoulders brushing against mine, and I jumped. Paul Morel. He didn't know if he should kiss me. His wife joined him. She introduced herself while he stared into space. I politely held out my hand to her, *Anne Martin*. I felt a sudden urge to add, *A former lover of your husband's*, but all I did was wish them health and happiness. *And love*, I added, while I glanced at Paul. It must have been the champagne — anger raced down my spine, my pulse quickened, the love scenes ran through my mind as if I were watching a speeded-up film. On the living-room rug at my place, in an Ottawa hotel, in my office one evening during a snowstorm. Until the break-up, the inevitable break-up. Already five years ago.

His wife chatted away while I sensed he was looking at me, stealing glances. Someone bumped into him. His arm almost imperceptibly grazed mine, and almost imperceptibly I quivered at his touch. The body always remembers what lies buried beneath the anger, beneath the disappointment, the resentment. His body remembered too. Surprised, he looked at me, took a step backwards. Time stood still. Then I felt Alessandro's arm around my waist. Instantly, Paul's body retreated into an old layer of memories, where there were no smells or colours. I made the introductions. *Paul Morel*. Spitefully, I added, *His wife, Claire*. *Alessandro Moretti*. A hint of sulkiness crept into Paul's expression. Did he really think I was going to mourn him for the rest of my life?

Alessandro was now talking to Paul as though he'd just been reunited with a long-lost friend. Paul, a taciturn man, hung on to his every word. And his wife was asking questions. Alessandro answered with all the graciousness he was capable of. Who could ever have predicted this scene? It seemed to be lifted from some second-rate novel. I did my best to keep a straight face. Now you've got your revenge, Anne Martin, I said to myself. Yes, you do. And to think you didn't even want to come to this party. You should have forgiven him, though. You are spiteful, Anne Martin. Yes, spiteful. But you're alive.

12

Sarai con mio. I say these words as I open the door. Alessandro corrects me, *Sarai con me, Anne.* I repeat the sentence so his native tongue might get used to my mouth, so it will flow one day like a sweet, hot drink. I add, *Ti bacio,* as I close the door. I go back over the few phrases he has taught me, all of them terms of endearment — he is the only one with whom I can speak Italian. It's crazy to learn a foreign language for a man, for him alone. It's love, passionate love. Alessandro leaves tomorrow. From then on, I'll only have the lingering echo of his voice in my ear. Will his words succeed in becoming so embedded in my flesh that he himself will live in me, with his smells, his hands, the taste of his skin in my mouth?

Not a soul on the street. Then a man appears on the other side of the lobby's picture window. He is running, his beard frozen, his eyebrows covered in frost, his breath spiralling upwards in front of his lips. I button up my collar, cover my face with my scarf. I am a faceless woman. We have to go out-side. I am gripped by the cold, it enters my nostrils, travels down to my chest. I could easily become frozen stiff. Fortunately, the market is only five minutes away. Alessandro would never get used to living here — who could? Just this morning a homeless man was found dead in a park. His corpse

was on the front page of all the daily papers, as though it were
simply a news item. But then again, would I be able to get used
to the constant noise of Rome?

And yet last night, when the city's street lamps came on,
together with the Christmas decorations and the neon lights,
Alessandro said, *This is home for me now.* It sounded like, *I love
you.* I went to join him in front of the window. I leaned my
head against his shoulder to watch the city, and watch love
suddenly alive in the city, love and the city inextricably linked,
two bodies that had finally found one another. For a fleeting
moment I saw the woman's smile, then it disappeared. Now
words exist that can erase the woman's lips. I would only need
to be told, *This is home for me now,* and I would be able to walk
through empty space.

Alessandro ran his hand over my skin. I trembled from
head to foot, trembled in the very marrow of my bones.
Silently we moved closer to each other, his hard sex against
my dress, his hands on my breasts. I pressed my mouth against
his mouth, his breath became my breath. I undid his belt. I
pulled him down on the rug with me, I wanted him to thrust
violently into the core of my flesh. I wanted him to enter me.
To let himself go. I held him tightly, like a vise. I dug my nails
into his buttocks while he ravaged me, and I screamed. I
screamed with every cell in my body. I screamed as a woman
screams when she is possessed by a man. I screamed as a
woman screams when a man says, *This is home for me now,* and
she hears in that phrase, *I love you.* What did we know about
the future? Very little, but Alessandro loved me. For once in
my life a man would have loved me.

13

He set his luggage down in the tiny hallway. He came back, walked over to the French doors, and then stood watching the city for a long, long time without saying a word. I left him alone with the winter as it swirled down before his eyes. Big, soft, insubstantial flakes landed on the window pane. Then there was a banging on the door. I frowned. Fanny was here — Alessandro had asked her to come to the airport with me. So I wouldn't be all alone right after he left.

Grudgingly, I let her in. That was it, from now on we wouldn't have a single private moment. But before me stood a brown-haired girl, dressed without even a hint of flashiness — a black woollen coat, a scarf that was too dull for her. I shouted, *Fanny, why?* Her familiar pealing laugh rang out. She walked towards Alessandro to ask for his opinion, he gave her an admiring look. Fanny plopped herself down on the sofa and told us her story. Étienne Langlois had chosen her to act in a film he was getting ready to shoot at the college. *The script is awesome*, she said ecstatically. After the airport, she would meet Étienne. She wanted to take me along, we would all go for a beer, I would be able to tell them what I thought about the script — hadn't I done some acting during my college days?

The gloom had vanished. All it had taken was Fanny showing up, and each and every thing had regained its true meaning. The leather chair, hollowed out a little bit by Alessandro, the smell of tobacco, now embedded in the furnishings, the Mozart sonatas which we didn't even bother putting back in the small cabinet any more. Alessandro lit his pipe, *One last smoke*, he explained while looking at me tenderly, then he would be able to leave peacefully. He would come back as soon as possible. Or else I would join him in Rome, or at Carthage, what did it matter? Weren't all cities alike when the one we loved was waiting for us?

Part III

1

That vise inside my chest, the night gripping me tightly, like a pair of arms. I burst into tears when I got home, I allowed myself to cry, something I never do. I looked at your empty chair and strained to hear your last words again. I picked up our Mozart sonatas from the table, put them into the CD player. They rang out, while the aroma of pipe tobacco still hung heavily in the air. Then I collapsed in my usual spot on the sofa and had a sudden vision of Mama, sitting in the living room, opposite Papa's empty chair. I was getting ready for work, I kissed her, but she barely responded. She must have been picturing Papa with Eileen, his smile, his gestures, his lips, as he used to be with *her* for all those years. I'm not picturing anything, I don't want to know about anything. About Papa's new wife, Papa's new house, or Eileen's son who has become Papa's son, *You'll see, he's adorable.*

I've never set foot in Papa's house. I vowed never to cross that threshold. I've seen little Michael only once and take great pride in that. It was in Montreal, shortly after the divorce. Papa had phoned me at the office where I was working as a trainee. He and Eileen were on their way to the seaside in Maine, they were inviting me out to a restaurant. I really don't know why I gave in.

I've forgotten the name of the restaurant, the street too. I think it was a Greek place that seemed to be suffocating beneath a jungle of climbing plants. An owner with bushy eyebrows took me to Richard Martin's table. I stood rooted to the spot for a few seconds, unable to bring myself to sit down. Could that man who was feeding a piece of bread to that insignificant little boy really be my father? But immediately he looked up, smiled at me, came towards me. I had to endure everything at once. The excessive sweetness of Eileen who even ventured a few words in French, little Michael's questions, and the glass of milk he spilled on the tablecloth. I saw Papa mopping up the damage without getting impatient. I almost said, *You weren't quite so patient with me*, but I fixed my gaze on a landscape on the wall. It was Delphi, immersed in a dazzling light. It was easy to understand why people used to go there to seek advice from the oracle. What would Pythia say to me, I wondered. It didn't take an oracle, though, to realize that Papa had placed his torch on another altar. Mama would have to be persuaded to dry her tears.

How old is Michael now? I've never asked Papa. On the rare occasions when I see him, I tell him how Mama is getting along. She's as good to Anna as ever, I will say. She's still beautiful, you know. I dwell on this, I hammer it in, even though a voice in my head keeps repeating, you can be awfully hard, Anne Martin. My kindness stays curled up deep inside me like a faithful dog, it will only go towards those it loves.

The music has died away without me even noticing. I should stir myself, put another disc into the CD player, make myself something to drink, a cup of herbal tea, run a bubble bath, move my feet, lift up my arms, unclench one of my hands, stretch out the fingers one by one, I should fight against the night. I should, but I can't. I sink into the darkness until it swallows me. I'm going to sleep right here, on the sofa, without getting washed. I'll wake up tomorrow with mascara smudges around my eyes and ghastly breath, like a woman who isn't looking for love. By then, you will have arrived in your other city, you'll sleep in your large empty bed, you'll dream, perhaps you'll mistake me for Jasmina. I try to dismiss that thought. Before going through the security gate, you hugged me very close while you said to Fanny, *You'll tell Anne every single day that I love her, won't you?* She shrugged, *Why should I? Isn't that obvious?* Alessandro's hearty, irresistible laugh rang out. He picked up his bag and airily blew me one last kiss, as if he were only going to the bakery on the corner.

Alessandro's laugh is suddenly in the room. Your deep laugh, Alessandro, and the night relaxes its grip, it lets me move, what time is it? Eleven o'clock. You have already been served a lukewarm meal, you've grimaced and asked for another bottle of red wine. You're drinking it slowly while listening to a bad recording of some symphony. You are thinking of me. Yes, I want to believe you are thinking of me at this very moment. I'm going up to the swimming pool, I'll probably be alone up there, and I'm going to dive as I used to when I was a girl, then I'll slowly come back up to the surface and swim, I'll swim on and on, all the way across the ocean, I'll go and join you in Rome, I'll go and sleep in your arms.

2

It isn't snowing, there's no wind blowing. The window displays only a motionless, watery sky. I walked. I cleaved through the air as if I were breasting high waves. For a brief moment I wanted to stop at Alessandro's favourite café, but I kept going, I had to keep going, I needed to get back to the life I led before. I pushed the building's door open by leaning against it with all my weight. On the register, I entered my name, the time, my office number. Without thinking. I recognized the slightly mouldy smell of the elevator, the odour of the freshly washed carpets in the corridor, then the aroma of Jean-Bernard's cigarette. I wouldn't be alone in the office. Too bad.

He came over and kissed me. He felt like talking, he started to tell me things. I listened with only half an ear, then I asked a question. Jean-Bernard answered, and lo and behold, I laughed, I shook with laughter without wondering what time it was in Rome. Before me, there was now only Montreal, tall and frozen, with Jean-Bernard's figure in the foreground. He was anxious to hear what I'd thought of his new lover. I came out with all the superlatives everyone who is in love wants to hear. Jean-Bernard smiled blissfully, and I ended up smiling too. What we call love, is it really anything more than boundless gullibility?

And how about Alessandro? For quite a while I said nothing. What words could possibly be strong enough? Finally I sighed, *This time it's not a married man.* Jean-Bernard burst out laughing. He wanted to know everything. So I told him. About Alessandro, Jasmina, and Marco, and Gianni. Jean-Bernard listened, looking pensive in the thin sunlight. *There are so many characters in your story.* I answered, *Never mind, I'm taking a chance on love.* I could hear Alessandro's deep, hearty laugh. I had a feeling I wasn't making a mistake.

3

It was like releasing a pigeon with its message. I tried to imagine myself somewhere outside the flow of time, waiting for a letter that never came, and I looked at the word *Send* on the screen with a great sense of relief. I clicked twice. The words embarked upon their journey, how many relays would it take before they reached Alessandro in his sleep? He's asleep right now, alone in his large bed, perhaps he is dreaming. Very soon, he'll be waking up, just as I am dropping off to sleep — alone, too, in my large bed. I will dream about him, about his hands on my skin. In the middle of these calculations I sometimes stop, raise my eyes towards the window and see him hovering in the icy air, over the frozen river, or he is spinning around in a sunbeam. He lightly touches my shoulder with a lingering finger, slides down my black silk strap. He caresses my breasts. It's dizzying, but not in a way that makes women topple over balcony railings. It is the exquisite kind of giddiness that makes the body ache with yearning. That's what I wrote to him.

One day I'll be able to write my letters in Italian. On my way home from work I bought a language course. I sat down in my usual spot on the sofa, put the tape in the cassette player and repeated after the instructor's voice all the phrases from the first lesson. *Prima lezione*. I mispronounced every word, put the accents in the wrong places. You would have laughed, Alessandro. I have no ear for music, I've always thought with my eyes and my hands. If you had been here, I would have been ashamed, since you speak my language so well. It was Jasmina's second language, I have to admit. You see, I am now able to say, *That woman was there before me.*

Terza lezione. I waited, still in my spot on the sofa facing your chair. I tried to think only of you. When I came home, there was a message from Mama on my voice mail. She spoke a little bit too fast, as when the world is turning the wrong way. It was about Anna — I understood that right away. What had happened? I tried to call her but came up against her answering machine, so the waiting began, just like a maze — you walk around and around in your head and you can't escape. You imagine things, you imagine the worst, what could it be? Anna insulting the caretaker of the building where she lives, Anna hitting the woman next door, Anna raving. Anna stepping out naked onto the balcony of her tiny apartment. Anna, her face smashed on the asphalt of the street. All I had left was your language, Alessandro. *Quarta lezione.* It wasn't until I had reached the fourth lesson that the phone finally rang. I dropped my phrasebook on the floor. Trembling, I picked up the receiver. Mama's voice sounded almost calm again. A sudden weakness. Anna was in her bed, unable to move. Mama had had to telephone the caretaker, ask him to unlock the door, call an ambulance. Now Anna was smiling on her stretcher in the corridor of the emergency department. Everything was fine, Mama kept saying, they were going to examine her tomorrow. Would I let my father know? Everything wasn't as fine as she let on. I kept my irritation to myself. I would telephone Toronto.

Eileen picked up the phone on the first ring. She spoke in French to mollify me. Papa wasn't home yet, a board of directors meeting. I almost added, *Or a mistress.* But I managed to put a wall between my spitefulness and me. In an icy voice I explained the situation. Papa would call me back the moment he walked in the door. The night would be spent waiting, I might get as far as the tenth lesson. By the time I went to bed, I would know how to make a reservation for a hotel room, I'd be able to order a meal in a restaurant, buy train tickets. Was there a lesson for the hospital? But soon the ringing of the phone drowned out the Italian. I glanced at my watch. Half past nine, it really had been a board of directors meeting. I wouldn't be lucky enough to see Papa being unfaithful to Eileen. Even so, there was no need to give up hope. For a man of sixty-five, Richard Martin could be considered handsome. His skin hadn't been burned by the Carthage sun. He was distinguished-looking, too. On those rare occasions when we went out for a meal together, women turned around to stare at him as he went by. Yet tonight his voice sounded weary. Or perhaps he was worried. But was he capable of that?

Once again, I went over everything. I did exaggerate — how Mama had been there all the time, how devoted she was, what a noble character she had. My words struck against a solid block, a rigid mass in the dark. Then I heard after a sigh, *Yes, your mother's very taken up with Anna.* He was admitting it. I hoped he would have trouble falling asleep. Let him think about Mama for just one night, sheltered as he was from all grief in his gilded cage, fragrant with the scent of English soap. I was going to dream of wild fits of rage, savage enough to rip through the smooth surface of the heavens. I was going to have that expression on my face that I didn't want Alessandro to see.

My hand still shook when I hung up. Was I becoming just as crazy as Anna? Anna's rages. Anna's violence. Words whispered in the night when I was supposed to be asleep in my pink bedroom. I would open the door a crack, I listened in. Sometimes they were telephone conversations, I needed to fill in the blank spaces, as in my exercise books at school. On evenings when the streets smelled of lilacs, Grandpapa would prolong his walk a little bit, he would arrive at the time when the sun has already vanished into the ground. Quietly, he would slip into my room so he could plant a kiss on my forehead. Then he'd go and drop into Papa's easy chair by the living-room window. As he did that night when I heard him cry, right after he'd said the word *asylum*. So as not to forget it, I repeated, *Asylum asylum asylum*. It sounded like a word from Sunday Mass, *Assumption*.

When I got up the next day, Mama was already at the hospital. At the breakfast table, Papa had his sleepless-night look, this was not a good time to bother him. He finally got up — the baby-sitter had arrived, I could ask her my question. She thought about it, then her face brightened. *An asylum is a place where people live who've taken a vow of silence*. There was no need for me to worry. My aunt was going to a convent.

4

With its windshield wipers swaying to and fro — they look just like heavy eyelids — the bus grips the road. I am afraid. I have picked a seat near the emergency exit and keep telling myself that the driver knows his job, but I can't help it, I am afraid. There is hardly any light coming in, it lurks behind a gradually thickening curtain of froth, made up of tiny white insects that stick to the glass. Framed by the window, a tow truck is lifting a car from a ditch. What a day to die.

My voice must have sounded as icy as Papa's when Mama woke me up this morning. Cardiac arrest, Anna was in a coma, the day was off to a good start. Get a hold of yourself, Anne Martin. It wasn't Mama's fault. Even Papa realized that. All right, I would telephone Toronto again, I would get both him and Eileen out of bed, she could count on me. I was going to hurry, I would arrive in Quebec City by noon. What a stroke of luck all the same, nothing urgent at the office, I only needed to give Jean-Bernard a quick call and I'd be off, I'd be on my way back to my childhood. To the life of a child born on the right side of the world. Bread on the table every day, chocolate at Easter, ballet lessons, and the piano lessons with Mademoiselle Grimard, a world made for good little girls. Of course there was an aunt who had gone away to a convent in an ambulance, the baby-sitter says it's just not possible, but I'm sticking to it, I heard *ambulance*, and *injection*, and *electric shock treatment* the other day in the kitchen, when Mama was talking with Papa. *Electric shock treatment* — the baby-sitter doesn't know what that is, she's promised to ask her mother. Now I am afraid of convents.

The bus gasps, snorts, grinds, splutters. A furrow has appeared between the driver's eyebrows. He tries to read the sky, just as the augurs of ancient Carthage would read the entrails of animals. I am not the only one who is worried. The tension among the travellers is palpable, you can feel it rising and rising. There's that battle-axe near me telling her troubles to a woman who is too polite to ask her to be quiet. Behind me, a man is showing off, while I stare at the white ghosts hovering beyond the window. I am trying to frighten them, I want them to calm down, retreat to their big clouds and go back to sleep. I want them to let us arrive safe and sound.

What time is it in Rome? Four o'clock. I am strolling along a grand boulevard, dazzling sunshine, I am wearing a fall coat, light ankle boots, we are doing our shopping in Italian. This evening we're having Gianni over, Jasmina's beloved son, he has come all the way from Florence. I will mollify him, yes I will, he is going to accept me. Last night he smiled in my dream, that was a good omen. He loved my pasta, he wanted to take me to the movies. I meant to say yes in Italian, but the phrase formed in English. I had Eileen's nasal voice, and her mouth, her nose, all the features of her face. You were looking at me in horror, Alessandro. Gianni started to shout, *That woman has killed my mother.* You didn't tell him to be quiet, you said nothing, you kept looking at me with those unfamiliar eyes, you let your son insult me. Fortunately, it was Papa who answered this morning, I wouldn't have been able to talk to Eileen.

Two honks. Two more honks in reply. We crane our necks, even the battle-axe who chatters on and on about her family problems, or perhaps she makes them up as she goes along — it's just like a soap opera. The man behind me heads towards the driver, he's going to find out what is going on, giving himself the air of a news reporter. We wait. He returns with a broad smile. The bus is now following the snowplow, we'll get there, we'll be late, but we don't need to worry any more. Well, not about the trip. Because the ghosts are grinning sardonically at the window, they'll accompany me to the hospital. I know I won't be able to shake them off.

5

I am inside a white eye, it keeps filtering everything. The walls, white and bare, displaying only a crucifix, a white Christ. The white bed with white sheets, and the spotlessly white pillow. The white window, and the street, and the city, and the river. The day, bleached white by the snow that falls and falls. At the end of the wires and tubes attached to her, Anna is asleep. Her white breathing. Her whitened brain finally cleansed of its voices. *Destroyed*, said the doctor. Death is waiting, I wait along with it, but I know it won't come today. It hovers at the window, with its candles, its homilies. What will the priest find to say about Anna's life?

Papa won't get here today, unless the pilot has taken leave of his senses. He has been saved yet again. Tonight he will sleep in Eileen's arms. Tomorrow, he'll come into the room relaxed and nicely turned out, he will give us an absent-minded peck on the cheek while casting an absent-minded glance at the heap of flesh covered with white linen, he'll order that she be disconnected from the life support equipment in the same tone of voice one uses when asking one's secretary for a file. From deep inside my white eye, I am going to watch Anna's life ebb away. Were you with Jasmina, Alessandro, when her eyelids closed for the last time on the infinite whiteness of eternity?

It is the hour when the stars appear in the windows of Rome. Gianni has enjoyed the meal you cooked for him, just like when he was a little boy. You are having your coffee, you step out on the balcony, you point your finger at the planets — you have done that so many times in Carthage. You are searching for the right words to tell him about me. Or perhaps you have chosen dessert time. In that case he silently gazes at the sky, he is a betrayed son. Or he has stormed out, shouting that he would never accept me. I try to tuck this thought away beneath other scenarios. Easter time, Rome, Marco, his wife, your grandson. And Gianni adores me, why wouldn't he love me? After all, it's either me or some other woman. It isn't good for a man to be alone, he needs a mate, God has said so.

Anna has been alone all her life, no one has ever touched her. Her body forsaken — a sapless tree, a parchment scorched by the sun, an old weathered hide, rose petals left behind between the pages of the first romance novel we've ever read, under the covers with a flashlight. And yet, how sensual Anna would look when she lowered her eyelids ever so slightly while rolling a mouthful of Cinzano around under her tongue. She was cheerful at home on Sundays, she loved to tell stories, she would say, *Before*, without being more specific. One day, time had simply stopped, there had been the illness, an earthquake or a tidal wave, one of those catastrophes you can't foresee that destroy everything in their wake — towns, forests, even the ice sheets in dried-up riverbeds. Yes, she would tell stories, she'd put on a velvety smooth voice when she said to Papa, *Do you remember?* Papa would laugh. Sometimes he'd add a detail, the colour of the bicycle or the lace on the surplice he used to wear when he served mass.

Papa laughed, Mama was happy. At night, in the car, as we watched Anna go into the building where she now lived, Mama always said, *Isn't it a miracle what that treatment has done?* Papa would agree listlessly, he must have been daydreaming about his next trip to Toronto. Did he already know Eileen when I bled for the first time? Anna's womb had dried up a long time before, nothing had withstood the great derangement, neither her mind nor her insides. Her body and soul had knitted together like Jesus and His cross. She had forgotten about the fragrant air of springtime, slinky silk dresses, thick hair streaming over her shoulders in the breeze on balmy evenings, when boys stroke girls' knees in movie theatres.

Anna had had sweethearts. That man we met one day at a restaurant. He had looked away so he wouldn't have to say hello to us — I had seen him in a photo taken by some lake. He has his arm around Anna's waist, he is staring at the camera with the look of a man who desires a woman. She knows it, she's agreeable, her lips parted a tiny bit. I swear that man has kissed her. He hasn't entered her, though. She still has a girl's eyes, tender talk is enough to make her happy, she is eighteen years old. How old is Papa? He is seven. A gorgeous little boy with his long, blond curls. Dressed as a tiny St. John the Baptist, he looked simply adorable in the St. Jean Baptiste Day parade, perched on a float with his white sheep. The crowd wouldn't stop clapping, Grandmamma said. He must have got his passion for the theatre right there on that day.

There will be no more bread for Anna, not ever. Drop by drop, the intravenous solution seeps into her arteries, to make us wonder a little more about life. This is probably her last night. Jasmina's last night. One day, it will be my last night, too. Who is going to be with me? Neither Mama nor you, Alessandro. You will have returned to the red earth of Carthage. Papa will be buried next to Eileen. But for now he is very much alive. He'll be here tomorrow, it can't go on snowing forever. I can already picture the look in his eyes as he approaches that collection of tubes and white sheets. How long has it been since he has seen his sister? Or Mama? The last time they found themselves face to face was before an indifferent judge. So many divorces, always the same hatred, the same demands, the same wrangling between the lawyers. At least the child was grown-up, she could look after herself, she was already at university. A brilliant girl, she is going to do well, you'll see. She doesn't have her mother's dreams — a husband, a house — she'll never shed any tears, she will never have huge dark circles under her eyes stretching all the way to her chin.

Tomorrow we will gather for one last family scene. We won't take any pictures. Together, but locked inside our individual loneliness, we will watch death claiming its own.

6

Darkness looms — a dense mass, a rampart of ice against the four walls. It holds me captive in the presence of a shadowy form who will be oblivious to me until the final surge of blood ebbs from her heart. The shadow stops me from getting up, approaching the bed, slipping my arms around that white bundle and shaking it to make it talk to me, finally talk to me. Talk to me, Anna, tell me how the mind breaks down one day, how it is destroyed, becomes pitted with holes and trenches growing larger and larger, how words vanish into the depths of a despair we won't recover from. And tell me about the fear. I know how afraid you have been, Anna. I know how fiercely we suffer when the soul that rules us is too intense. You fought as hard as you could, then one day you joined the ranks of the vanquished.

It's not my fault, Anna, if I am stronger than you are. It isn't my fault. *I* never gave up. Even when things came apart inside my head, I went forward by putting one foot in front of the other. By some miracle, I was able to keep going. I have staked out my little territory, I have drawn houses where people can be safe, warm houses where they can love, and laugh, and die quietly in their sleep at a ripe old age. Like Alessandro's house in Tunis. But there are never any guarantees. Jasmina died in hospital after much suffering. You were there, Alessandro, you watched over her. You weren't thinking about me yet. Was she? Does one think in one's dying moments about the woman who will take our place?

A light touch, almost a caress — the nurse brushes against my arm, I should go to bed, Anna isn't aware of anything any more, what's the use of sitting up all night with her? But I insist with all the stubbornness I am capable of. I have decided to stay here, and that's what I will do. One never knows — in the still of the night an angel may come by, spread around a little bit of peace, put my mind at rest. I will settle Anna on its wings, she will quietly fly away. At least this once I will have shown her some kindness without expecting anything in return. Because she cannot answer me from deep inside her suspended world. I no longer exist, neither does Mama, nor Papa, whom she always loved so much. I will stay here until she dies, in an everlasting glacial night, patiently groping for words to sustain me.

You may not be asleep either. Perhaps you woke up with a start, your heart beating wildly. In your dream, Gianni tore up my photograph before slamming the door. You are shaking, shaking all over. You are afraid, too, but it isn't like a sudden dizzying plunge that might be the end of you. In *your* world there are causes and effects, whys and wherefores. The bright blue sky, not dimmed by mists of snow. One can see clearly into the distance. Where you are, one can learn how to make vases speak, even when a single tiny shard is all that is left.

A soft rattling sound. I jump. I must have dozed off. A figure is bent over the ghost in the bed, the night nurse this time, a friend of Mama's. She comes towards me, two o'clock, I should go home, no one's love can do anything for Anna. I blush. I can't very well say to her, *It isn't love — only the need to understand.* Anna's madness is the last remaining mystery of my childhood, I've cleared up all the others. Santa Claus visiting everyone's house in a single night, the existence of God in three persons, the resurrection of Jesus. But I could never stop believing in Anna's madness. It was a raw, true fact, with rages and fits, electroshock treatments, psychiatrists. And fear on certain nights, when I'd wound up alone in Los Angeles, with the feeling I was walking on a tightrope — one little step, one tiny step, and bang! you topple over, you have crashed to the ground. I never told you, Alessandro. Would you still love me? Even now, the night can be hell, just like that painting by Hieronymus Bosch, those monsters and devils, and I never know if I am going to be able to escape. Then I have to play dead. I wait for dawn. The earth always ends up turning again. I know this even when I don't know anything else any more. It is my most fundamental truth.

Fear. Fear that corrodes the words inside my mouth. Fear is an animal buried alive in the silence of the night. This is something you will never be able to understand, Alessandro. Even when you are shaking, even when your body heaves with sobs, all the words, I'm sure, still fit together in your sentences. Even during Jasmina's final moments. Together with your sons, you knelt down before her, you recited prayers — you believe in rituals. I don't. For me, stone is simply stone, people don't build a Church, only structures. In this room, someone is dying with a frozen brain, bleached white by the cold, she has forgotten everything. Even the jumble of voices that spun their web beneath her skull. Yet I am here, I watch over Anna, I'll watch over her until the first light of dawn, I'll be with her while she lives through her final night. I will only leave her when I am certain she is taking away with her the full sweep of her madness.

7

Truth is stranger than fiction. A man who has gone missing in the war turns up forty years later. A woman declared dead starts to shout at the morgue when people try to move the bier under her coffin. Papa has always loved stories like that. He has an incredible imagination. Also an incredible lack of sensitivity. Today, he succeeded in getting me to argue with Mama. *For goodness' sake, Anne, try to understand.* I yelled just like Anna on one of her bad days. I grabbed my coat and rushed out without my hat or my gloves.

Fortunately, the night is blissfully mild. A golden moon tries to break through the clouds. I turn up the collar of my coat and straightaway a feeling of good will washes over me. Not the urge to forgive. Certainly not. I won't forgive Richard Martin. A kind of patience, rather, causing one to look at things differently, a calming down, a twitch of amusement hovering at the corner of one's lips. Like the subtle smile I caught on Mama's face when Papa told us that Eileen had come to Quebec City with him. In a single stride I bounded across the eight floor tiles between my chair and the window to go and fasten my eyes on the post-blizzard scenery. A snow-blower was spouting snow into huge identical trucks, there were ten of them, I counted them and recounted them to slow down the fluttering of my heart. Mama didn't have a chance to comment on Papa's charming announcement — the nurse had come in. The doctor was going to arrive in a couple of minutes, they were going to proceed. I couldn't help laughing maliciously. Proceed — that's what they say when they want to dispatch decent people into the next world. But I didn't have time to be shocked or feel pity, or to wonder about the white blotches on Papa's cheeks.

Everything began to happen in a great rush — the doctor's arrival, the explanations, the gestures, Mama laying her hand over Anna's, Anna's heart that kept on beating all by itself, thump thump thump, Anna saying no, she refused to die, Anna putting up a fight even though it didn't make any sense. She alone would decide when she was going to die. I was proud of her, yes I was — proud that people would sometimes mistake me for that crazy Anna. Mama, like all good nurses, remained stoical, while the white blotches on Papa's cheeks were turning red. His edifice was collapsing, now he would just have to wait it out, make trip after trip here. Hadn't they often seen patients survive for months, even years? *We can't very well strangle Anna.* I blurted this out in a soft voice, and Papa stared at me as if I were a monster. I thought, he has got out of the habit of acting. And then everything became clear. He hated me just as much as I hated him. The two of us were locked in a hatred as intense as love.

There is beauty in hatred, I am sure of that. One can walk down unfamiliar roads, learn new languages, rebuild one's house somewhere else. Whereas love shackles our feet to a ball and chain. Mama had insisted on keeping her house in a deserted state. She herself had never left, except to go down south with Anna. There is a spring in my step now. My anger is dying down, I don't feel as resentful towards Mama any more. But still just as resentful towards my father. How tactless of him to have come with Eileen! And Mama who, as always, defended him, *Try to understand, Anne.* Well, exactly, I refuse to understand, just as Anna refuses to die. I reject all those empty phrases sprouting from Mama's mouth — a jungle you get lost in, a prison you can never get out of. Not alive, anyway.

8

Someone had to make a decision. We couldn't wait for death day after day, hover over a motionless face, keep our eyes on the grey roots appearing in the dyed hair. I decided to go back to Montreal. I was abandoning Anna to her dreamless sleep, but what do we know? In limbo, where she is, she may be threatened, pursued, hunted down by harsh voices, white stones thrown at her body which can no longer defend itself. No one can help, I even less than the others. She stopped talking to me so many years ago I wouldn't be able to count them on the fingers of both my hands.

My homecoming from Los Angeles after studying there for a year. Anna and Mama are having a Cinzano in the living room as I set my luggage down in the hallway. Mama is crying when she kisses me, she offers me everything at the same time, Cinzano like them, coffee, a beer, cookies and milk. She is a mother again. I really have succeeded in surprising her. But Anna puts her glass down on the living-room table — a determined thump — she gets up, announces she is leaving. A migraine, she is going to eat in her own quiet apartment. No matter how much Mama protests, and suggests aspirins, an ice pack on her forehead, a short nap before the meal — I remember it perfectly — Anna strides towards the door and leaves without so much as a goodbye. Behind the screen door, I can make out a twirling flowered dress, the dress of a seductress on the shattered body of a shattered woman. That had been my last image of Anna Martin.

How could I have known that nearly twenty years later I would find her lying motionless in this bed? The next time I would see Anna, she was going to be inside a tiny urn, less richly decorated than the vases at Carthage. Ashes to ashes, dust to dust. No matter how often this is repeated to us, the teaching won't sink in. We never get used to it.

I quietly stood my luggage against the white wall of the room without noticing the figure in a navy blue jacket who was gently laying a face cloth over Anna's forehead. I only spotted Papa as I straightened up — his eyes, the kind of eyes he sometimes adopted when he looked at Mama in his previous life. Or perhaps, so as to be forgiven for my anger, I invented an actual, beating heart for him, a heart that gives, comforts, and looks after you. But the hand on Anna's temples was very real, it was the hand of a mature man, with clean nails, accustomed to a calculator and contracts. *You see, I'm not all that clumsy.* It didn't sound like a line in a play. I smiled at him while I slid a chair over to the bed. Anna's face formed a kind of blotch on the pillow, I had difficulty making out any human features. *Your aunt used to be so beautiful.* Papa's faint voice. And the uneasiness, the horror I had vaguely felt the last couple of times I had seen a great friend of Jean-Bernard's in the hospital, just before his death. But then you forget. I had forgotten.

Anna's temples. The water in the white enamel basin. The white face cloth flitting about in Papa's hands. I couldn't bear

to look at anything white any more. I tried to sound determined. I said, *I'm going back to Montreal.* Papa looked up. I
added, *I've got to go back to work.* Papa nodded absently. Eileen
was going back to Toronto, too. He himself would stay on for
a few days, and then he'd see. He sat there, a little stooped,
with the creased face of someone who hasn't had enough sleep.
In his eyes there was a worry I couldn't identify.

Today, he wasn't a man you could hate. I just couldn't get
up, I sat glued to my uncomfortable chair, I was no longer the
talented architect or Alessandro Moretti's lover, but only a
very small girl facing her father. I was waiting for a sign of love
which didn't come. Which wouldn't come. For the time being,
he delicately moved his hand, he belonged to a dead woman.
Perhaps I would need to die, but not completely. My body
breaking with a sharp snap, and yet surviving, for a few hours,
just long enough to receive a word of endearment, a last caress,
a kiss on the cheek. But I was very much alive, and my work
was waiting for me. I was the one who kissed his cheek.
Absentmindedly he said, *Goodbye, my girl,* remembering in
spite of himself that he was my father. Then he became Anna's
little brother again. My childhood now only existed on a few
rectangles piled up in Mama's cupboard, yellowing a little more
with each one of my birthdays.

9

I have turned my back on death the way one decides to turn one's back on love. Time suddenly explodes, splits into tiny pieces, millions of molecules — one is no longer trapped inside the present moment, we wind up somewhere else, hope for something else, we remember the words *yesterday* and *tomorrow*. All it took was a whiff of the air in the bus which reeked of ammonia and dust, then I picked out the cleanest window, stowed my bag in the luggage rack. I sat down, stretched out my legs, took possession of my life again. Once more, I had a vibrant body, I thought of you, Alessandro. Soon I would be switching on my computer, I would know your son Gianni's reaction. His disappointment, his anger, perhaps his hatred — I was ready now. He could scream or he could slap me, I wasn't going to give in.

I suddenly longed for you to be there, sitting next to me in the heavy air of this almost empty bus. You would caress me gently underneath my coat until the world converged in your hand, until all of reality dwelled in the space of the five fingers of your hand. Next, taking advantage of the fat man two rows behind us being asleep, I would undo the belt of your pants, my fingers would reach for your flesh, I would feel you becoming erect in spite of yourself. You'd say, *Stop*, but I would continue, you would harden, you would quiver, silently, your mouth slightly open. You'd pinch your lips a little bit to stifle your moaning, and you'd close your eyes, as the rhythmic throbs of the universe suddenly washed over you. My hand would be wet. No one could prevent me from loving you, neither the fat man nor your son. Or my aunt on her interminable deathbed.

Anna had had to give up all thought of this. Once madness took over, her whole world was contained in her head, a world of actors and actresses. She went to the movies every night, knew entire scenes from *Gone with the Wind* and *Casablanca* by heart, made Papa go over them with her. Sometimes, in a restaurant, they would repeat a complete dialogue. It was funny, Mama would wipe away a tear from the corner of her eye. Anna would take another sip of wine, she looked like a girl again, she returned from the dead. Anna's illness — a mystery, a novel, a game of hide-and-seek. An injustice.

The snow on the road sign hides the number of kilometres still left to go. Never mind. The bus flies, time flies, my day-dreams fly by faster than I want them to. You drenched my hand with your sperm, Alessandro, and suddenly I am back in a life stitched together with invisible thread. A life I don't know anything about. Not even the name of Anna's illness. Papa has forgotten, and I have never made any attempts to find out. Anna will die in the wake of an unnamed madness. But can some ancient Greek term help us to understand the confusion of madness? What remains is patience, Mama's endless patience, Mama listening to her talking about the voices, about the neighbours who are spying on her, and Mama's advice, *You've got to relax, Anna. Watch your favourite programmes tonight. Don't forget to take your medicine.*

Madness, death, Papa abandoning us. How can I make sense of it all, Alessandro? And love? There, at least, we don't ask questions. We move towards each other on a single tightrope, without asking ourselves if the net below has holes in it, we carefully put down our feet, we take our time. Gianni will accept me in the end. After all, he is a grown-up, he has his own life, his own friends, romances too, he must have loved other people besides Jasmina. You will have set an example, Alessandro, you will have made your way back to life. I, Anne Martin, will have done that — restored you to life. No one can possibly hold it against me.

10

I pressed my face against the window as if some heavenly being might come soaring down from the dreary sky to hold me. No one did. I was going to stay alone with my anger, my yearning, my confusion. I didn't even jump when Jean-Bernard walked in. *What are you doing there?* I said, *I'm trying to cry.* He laughed. Well, how about spending the evening together, we had been getting away from our pleasant routine lately, hadn't we? I said, *Just give me an hour, and I'll be all yours.* While blowing me a kiss, he replied, *That sounds promising.* He'd succeeded in extracting a smile from me. Why this sporadic need to act as though we might feel desire for each other, even when we both knew perfectly well we would never touch each other? This evening we were obviously going to be just as well-behaved as we always were. I thought I smelled Alessandro's tobacco and felt his lips tickling my cheek.

I miss you. Yesterday, your message began with those words. It also ended with those words. In between, it was all about your desiring me — you wanted me, right there, close to you. You barely mentioned Gianni. I thought, this is a good sign. I immediately fired off my reply, *When will we see each other again?* Just this one sentence. Why bother telling you the story of a dead woman who refused to die? On the sheets of paper in front of me, scale drawings stretched their vertical lines. I felt unable to make even the most trivial decision. *You are being so stupid,* Fanny would have said. I would have gone further than that. The more I was going to miss Alessandro, the stupider I was likely to become. And it wasn't my work that would hold me back! Scale drawings for stupid architects — that's what I had to deal with. Perhaps I should change professions. But I'd built up my life stone by stone, I wasn't going to destroy it all in a fit of the January blues. Fortunately, Jean-Bernard came back. The work could easily wait until the next day.

Outside, it was absolute hell. The temperature had suddenly dropped so low that thermometers cracked. People hesitated for a moment in doorways, they didn't dare step outside. But we would walk. The restaurant wasn't far. We would walk so we could feel the cold entering our lungs and spit it out again, a billowy plume of steam, a tiny act of defiance flung at the world. There was still some fight left in us. Luckily, a cosy fire was waiting for us at the back of the deserted restaurant, as was the owner with his southern verve. Another life now presented itself to people who didn't feel like spending the evening face to face with their loneliness.

I ordered a Moretti and got up to go and retrieve my voice-mail. I instantly recognized Papa, his neutral, reserved, smooth, everyday voice. *It's over.* My heart began to beat a little faster. We may expect someone's death, but that isn't the same thing as when it really happens. I played the message a second time, for no reason. *It's over.* If you listened closely, you could make out a kind of quavering in Papa's throat. So he wasn't always completely protected from everything.

11

The condolences, the thank you's, the contrite smiles. The occasional tear. Papa was giving a flawless performance. He introduced me to so many people it made my head spin — you'd think he'd never left Quebec City. I held out my hand, curled up my lips, flashed the tips of my teeth. I was Anne Martin, my father's daughter, his own flesh and blood, the child who would deservedly bear his name until his last breath. His other family, the one from Toronto, stood back a little bit. Perhaps Eileen sensed my indignation. But this was no time to make a faux pas. Then Eileen's son came towards me. He was a man now, he must have been twenty-six or twenty-seven, I quickly calculated. A man, yes, but with a lingering trace of boyishness in his manner, his gestures not quite adapted as yet to the occasion. He was anxious to tell me he was finishing his master's degree in architecture in April, he would really like to talk to me for a bit after the ceremony. Surely, this had to be some nasty practical joke. I felt dizzy all of a sudden, I leaned against the wall. Eileen had robbed me of everything, even the one thing I valued most.

Now the swirling was about to start. I took a deep breath, looked around for Mama. Together we walked up the aisle towards the small urn surrounded by gladiolas and carnations.

We sat down in the front pew, over to the left, while the other clan settled in the right-hand pews opposite us. Even though I didn't mean to, I took a quick peek at Michael. He was slipping into the second pew from the front, behind the others, as if all this didn't concern him. Who had insisted on him being there — Papa or Eileen? Mama kept very still. I drew myself up, I would hold myself straight, ramrod straight. I would fight against Papa's callousness, fight against the whole congregation as it dumbly mouthed the responses to the priest's prayers, fight against the anger surging up in my chest.

Was it sadness, or just the soft light from the stained-glass windows, but Papa looked shrunken all of a sudden, much older. When I turned my face a little bit, I caught a worried look in Michael's eyes. He had noticed, too. Worry, compassion, love — the ideas linked up with one another in my mind. The man kneeling in front of him was his father, too, even if he had nothing to do with his birth. Actually, there was a family likeness between them. With the passing years, they'd ended up looking alike — their bearing, their height, the way they combed their hair. Discreetly, I let my gaze wander from one to the other, and the urn became blurred, the flowers as well. I had to sit down. What if Michael really was Papa's son?

The priest launched into his homily. I tried to listen to what he said about Anna, but it was just like a silent film. He waved his arms about, put on serious faces and sad faces, but nothing got through to me. I was on the other side of a glass wall, busy doing some mental arithmetic. My age at the time of Papa's earliest trips to Toronto, the year he was transferred, the year of the break-up, Michael's age on the day when he'd knocked over his glass of milk at that restaurant. I followed the thread all the way to the end by trying to recall certain events, trivial incidents that might lead me to the exit of the maze. Everything fitted together but, still, that wasn't an answer, only Eileen and Papa could say yes or no. I glanced at Mama beside me. Had she ever indulged in these calculations during a sleepless night? For the moment, all her attention was riveted on the priest's words. She smiled, and I pricked up my ears. Anna had had the best life possible thanks to the presence of her family. I instinctively turned towards Papa — how often had he gone to see Anna after the divorce? His back seemed to be bending like a spoon. Guilt, no doubt. My lips spread into a smile, but it wasn't like Mama's. Mine was a malicious, gloating kind of smile.

I had felt the blood drain from my face the day before, when Mama told me Papa was going to show off his Toronto family at the funeral. Once again, a tidal wave had gushed from my lips, a rage too intense for me, shaking me to the very marrow of my bones. I had loudly wished all three of them would go to hell, Papa, Eileen, and Michael, along with Anna who was bringing us nothing but trouble, even now that she was dust. I had blamed Mama, she had never been able to stand up for herself. Cowardice, monumental cowardice, that's what forgiveness really was. Mama listened without contradicting me, keeping a nurse's composure.

And yet, behind the veil of incense the priest was asking us to be hopeful, one day we would be re-united with those who had left us. Papa had lowered his eyes, I wanted to believe he was thinking of Mama. But he turned around towards Eileen and slipped a word in her ear. She smiled that insufferable little smile of hers. Even after all the Last Judgements in the world, we would never, ever, be together again. Only priests still had hope and faith. The ceremony was over. I followed Papa and Eileen down the aisle, vowing I wouldn't bother coming to their funerals. Let Michael handle that job. The role of the dutiful son would be all his. I, Anne Martin, wasn't going to stir. I would stay home, without a scrap of feeling in my heart.

12

A furtive shadow, right there, near the curtain. And the muslin moves, it flutters, billows. The veil is about to part. Who will appear? Alessandro perhaps? But the shadow has vanished. Alessandro is asleep in Rome. There is only me here in the armchair, and the restless, troubled night. I must keep still, let my eyes wander around the room, wait a little longer, for the shadow, there, behind the muslin curtain. In the first year after the break-up, Papa would suddenly loom up before me like a ghost. He was coming back, he was choosing *us*.

Mama switches on the lamp. She puts the cups down on the table, settles into a chair. *That was quite a day, wasn't it?* I tuck my legs up against me, I don't respond. She doesn't seem to notice. She starts talking the way people do when they live alone and they happen to have someone sitting opposite them, she goes over the details of the funeral. I only half listen. Cousin Irène, a widow now, was there, so was her brother, everybody had made the effort to come, Papa had seemed to be delighted. I nod, while I'm pondering whether I'll ask my question. But I hear myself say, *Do you think Michael is Papa's son?* Dead silence. The air is totally still. The muslin curtain hangs motionless. The room feels cold. I'm sorry already. But then I can breathe again, I'm no longer sorry — is there ever a right time for the truth to come out? My voice sounds a little shaky as it begins to rise. I give the facts, I calculate, I link all the events just like coloured threads, they end up weaving a tapestry where even in the twilight you can detect the shape of things. Mama takes a sip of tea, she can only agree with me. Figures don't lie. All you have to do is add and subtract in order to arrive at a perfect understanding of the world. Beyond hunches or resemblances.

Strangely enough, Mama seems relieved. She, too, knows how to calculate. She is looking at a shimmering spot on the wall. Images must be flashing by in front of her eyes, but she isn't going to talk, I'll just have to imagine them. Papa's arms no longer open for her. Too tired, he says. That is actually why he has been travelling home less and less often from Toronto. She pretends to believe him — no, she really does believe him. When do you start admitting to yourself, my husband doesn't want me any more? You wait, you hope for the gesture that will calm your fears. It takes so little sometimes to make two bodies harmonize with the pulse of the world. Once more, you are a twosome, until the bed reveals its crack yet again, this time an even wider, deeper one. You go to sleep at night with your hand tightly clutching the sheet, you are afraid you may sink deep into nightmares that will trap you forever.

Another sip of tea. Another one, and another. The blood is warming up a little in our veins. But the words remain stuck in our throats, they won't puncture the silence. There will not be any miracle. Anna isn't a saint, just a madwoman slumbering inside her urn. She can't do anything for us. We've still got tea, music, sleep. And those little needles pricking my calves.

I should stretch my legs, stand up. I walk over to Mama, I stroke her arm. I say, *It's time to go to bed*. She snaps out of her daydream, she murmurs almost to herself, *I will miss Anna*. I blurt out, *But you're going to be free now*. She shrugs. I don't understand. Once again I refuse to understand. There are feelings that are simply too heroic for me.

Part IV

1

It's always Christmas here. Always Christmas lights when darkness gathers. The night sky in Carthage must be black, velvety black — no, more a sombre black, a swath of black cloth concealing the tombs. Alessandro can sleep in peace. No one will come and pillage. But is he asleep at this very moment? Perhaps he's dreaming on his balcony while having one last smoke. His eyes gaze into the darkness, he's looking for something, he's thinking of me. *Mi manchi, Anne. I miss you.* Before him, no man had ever said that. I immediately typed, *Mi manchi anche tu.* In the bedroom's shadowy light, desire devoured the screen. On its own, the sentence looked obscene, I needed to add things, weaken it a bit, talk about the Italian lessons that weren't going too well, find excuses — work, the funeral, Jean-Bernard has another unhappy love affair, life over here repeats itself like a movie scene that speeds up or slows down depending on the projectionist's mood.

I cooked his favourite dish last night and we talked until our eyelids drooped. Jean-Bernard slept in my bed, next to me. Would you understand, Alessandro? I didn't tell you. There are certain risks I don't want to take any more. I left my desire for you on the screen, raw, naked, and sent it along in that utter nakedness, as though I were spreading my legs in front of you, as though I were pleading, Take me, right here, right now. In the Christmas city, by the swimming pool.

A loud splash behind me. Drops on my back. I swing around. Fanny's bathing suit forms a red streak at the bottom of the pool. Then she slowly comes up, with that sensible hair of hers I just can't get used to. *I startled you again.* Her laugh echoing each time against the concrete wall. I laugh, too. No reprimands this evening. I simply ask, *What time do you have to leave?* But she's already far away, her arms rhythmically breaking the surface of the water, there she is holding on to the side of the pool before she comes gliding towards me. She gasps out, *Seven thirty.* On the wall, the hands of the clock point at the six. I slip on my robe, it's time to get dinner ready. Fanny will join me later.

Pitch-darkness in the rectangle of the doorway, a huge black screen. Here, no one misses me. But I put my finger on the light switch and the Phoenician gods materialize on the little table. I am no longer completely alone, the world is there, it exists, within reach. Just one more word of love from you, Alessandro, and the world would find a place inside my chest, it would beat to the rhythm of my blood. I head for the computer but stop short. No. One cannot spend all one's time in anticipation. Luckily, Fanny has just come in. *What's for dinner? Pasta.* Water runs down into the satiny stainless steel, a pinch of salt, a little oil, my gestures become focused once again. Then our casual talk, I let the words twirl around in the room. *Where is the screening going to be held? At Vincent's.* Just that name, and the past comes to life. Emma Villeray. Jérôme. Will his ghost be there tonight to comment on his son's film?

What is it you're thinking about? About you, Fanny, looking like such a well-behaved young lady, and Étienne, playing at being a film director, about Jérôme, who doesn't know anything about his son any more. He'd be surprised, the first sequences aren't bad at all. Fanny moves well, a young woman already when she tilts her head back, calling attention to the curves of her breasts. Has she made love with Étienne? The question keeps flitting through my mind. Amazing, isn't it, for a woman who has made love so many times without expecting any love at all? *What is it you're thinking about?* I must answer. I turn my eyes towards the vast expanse of twinkling city lights. I murmur, *Do you suppose there will be another message from Alessandro tonight?*

2

I lie in wait, for the cry of a child, a cheery voice on the television, a quarrel at the neighbours'. But it's useless, there isn't a sound, everything's dead — the table, the coverlet Mama has neatly folded up at the foot of the bed, the saucepan left behind on the stove, the lipsticks lined up like tiny gravestones on the chest of drawers. And the unwashed curtains, and the window, and the patch of dirty sky, and the rain digging deserted nests in the grey snow. I should move my legs, though. Walk over to the kitchen, get out a package of trash bags. Fill them, then tie them up. But I can't. My body has lost the ability to make sense of the orders I give it. Anna's anger if she knew I was here. When we are in the throes of death, do we give a thought to those green bags that will carry the left-over bits and pieces of our lives to the garbage? The apartment will be practically empty by this evening. On Monday, a charitable organisation is picking up the remaining furniture. Then Anna will only exist in our memory.

A sound, at last. Footsteps on the wood. Mama has just come in. *Which room will we do first? The bedroom.* Let's begin by closing up the place that holds the mysteries. Once that is done, we'll breathe easier. My image embeds itself in the mirror in front of me as I pull out the bottom drawer of the chest.

An Anna of long ago appears, the twenty-year-old, the Anna whose life still lies ahead of her. I take out the lacy underthings, the ones we buy with dreamy thoughts about the hands that will take them off. The prices are still on them, they've never been worn. A lump rises in my throat. I can still see Anna, enormous in her hospital gown, the grey roots of her dyed hair against the pillowcase. I take out the lace panties, the delicate silk half-slips. I put them on the bed with my fingertips, a little embarrassed. This is Anna's secret garden, her rosy image of the world, the longed-for future. I don't want to think about the love affair that only happened at the bottom of a drawer. I pull out the other drawers, I barely glance at the clothes, too small, too young-looking, cut too low at the front. I don't react when Mama tells me I can keep anything I like. No, no, I won't keep anything, I don't want to feel against my skin any fabric Anna has chosen, touched, put away, and scented with her bars of soap exuding fake lavender smells. No, no, I won't keep anything of Anna's.

Mama approaches with a stack of magazines. Diaphanous women stare out at us with unseeing eyes. Some aren't any older than Fanny. Or than Anna caught up in her impossible dreams, since her life had ground to a halt. Mama and I never knew that young woman, only Papa did. But he isn't here, he escaped once more. Voices nearly rose again last night at the house — why didn't Mama let him work it out with Eileen? Mama could have come and spent the weekend with me in Montreal, the two of us would have gone out, to the theatre, the movies, a restaurant. She shook her head with a smile, she really wanted to clear out the apartment herself, it was up to us, not Eileen or Papa, to separate Anna from her earthly life. It was a gesture we owed to her.

The furrow between Mama's eyebrows is back while she bustles about. The whole place is dirty, we'll have to clean it. Old dust under the bed, grease stains. The cleaning woman didn't do a very good job, Anna probably never even noticed. Mama blames herself. I don't try to reassure her, I wouldn't succeed. I am struggling to solve the riddle of her attachment to Anna. Look at the two of them, that photograph from their last vacation down south, arm in arm, two alien worlds touching each other. I put the small rectangle down in front of me without saying, *Please explain it to me.* How can you possibly explain love?

Mama and I have been sufficiently diligent, the bedroom is now empty. I close the door behind me. There, that's done. Lunchtime. I'm hungry. Mama suggests a little restaurant on the corner of the street. She used to go there with Anna, what a lovely memory. Another flash of anger. But I manage to speak quite calmly, I propose taking a short walk in the rain and going to a cosy café not far from here. We'll order a nice meal, we'll eat all by ourselves, just the two of us, we'll forget about Anna. We will learn to forget her.

3

It was no longer Anna's world. The space had closed on the everlasting silence of her voice. Mama wanted to walk through the living room one last time. She lingered for a moment by the rain-swept window. I felt a sudden urge to step forward and open it, flood the apartment with all the water in the sky. Everything would go mouldy, disappear beneath a layer of moss, fungi, bacteria. Nothing would survive Anna. Mama bent down, then stood up again with a slip of paper left behind under a piece of furniture, and I caught the emotion in her voice as the words resonated against the walls. *Carrots, bread, ham, milk, soap, toothpaste.* I felt a tightness in my chest. I was close to tears, though I hadn't cried either at the hospital or the church. I went up to Mama. I took the small rectangle of folded paper in my hands, I wanted to reread the last words we had left of Anna's, true words expressing being hungry, thirsty, and eager to triumph over death for one more day, one more year, one more decade. Then I folded up those words and slipped them into my pocket without asking Mama if she might like to have them. Fanny would say, *You're being stupid,* but some stupid words are more beautiful than poetry.

Mama stared out of the window again at a city held captive behind shafts of rain. Or perhaps she imagined flowers on the dirty glass, small crosses, needle marks in Anna's pale arm at the hospital. Or her own pale arm. One day, it would be *my* pale arm. But right now we needed to stow away our grief, our memories, go off to a movie. Slowly, like a sleepwalker, Mama followed me to the door. A man said hello to us as we left, probably the same one Anna heard when she imagined voices. What could he possibly have been accusing her of? I repeated just to myself, *Carrots, bread, ham, soap, toothpaste.* Those words were what I wanted to keep of Anna's.

The caretaker was there, behind the window of his office. He agreed to unlock the apartment on Monday morning for the people who were supposed to pick up the furniture. I said to Mama, *You won't need to come back.* Hesitantly Mama handed over the key. I opened the door onto the raw chill of dusk. Mama followed me, reluctantly. I had rushed her but didn't feel guilty. Someone had to sprinkle a last handful of earth over Anna's dead body.

4

Did the man really look like Alessandro? Maybe not. All he did was walk by our table with that pungent smell from his jacket, and time suddenly opened like Carthage's red earth. Against my will, the words took shape in my mouth. Yet I'd solemnly promised myself I wouldn't tell Mama anything. Vowed I wouldn't share Alessandro with her. But I did, I told her everything, in one go. How we met in Tunis, him staying with me in Montreal, his trip to Carthage with a group of students. Then Jasmina, Marco, Gianni. I actually almost uttered the phrase that had set me dreaming in front of my screen, *Mi manchi*. Yes, I talked, feeling a bit ashamed, like a girl who can't keep a secret. But the waiter arrived with the dessert menu, we were whisked back into a safer life, one with tiny decisions. Nothing momentous could possibly happen to us that night at this table, in a restaurant jam-packed with tourists who had come to celebrate exactly what, I don't know. The carnival was still a long way off. I chose the apple tart. Mama remained silent. Then she said in her motherly voice, *Be careful, Anne. Please be very careful*. I lowered my eyes. Why had I hoped Mama would understand? Now she was going to worry. A foreigner. Almost as old as Papa. A widower, with children on top of that. It was an unrealistic dream, I was beginning to be like that crazy Anna with her lacy underwear and her life lived entirely between the covers of magazines.

The waiter brought the desserts, but I pushed my plate away. I heard Mama ask, *Aren't you eating?* I replied, *I'm not hungry any more.* It was a logical, plausible answer. Mama smiled, I was getting back to things that really mattered, the body revealing its vital needs. I watched Mama silently eat her piece of cake, in tiny, careful, methodical bites. No, Anna's death hadn't settled anything. I fought back little-girl tears and went to pay the bill despite Mama's protests. Around the cash, there was a joyful commotion, a group of young Anglophones, and I wondered if Michael was spending the evening with his pals or with a girl-friend. I tried to picture him, but it was Eileen's face that continually loomed up before me. I scowled. As for Papa, he'd be watching some television programme in his British-style *drawing-room*.

The rain had finally stopped. Heavy snow, festive snow, clung to the scenery. The old city was beginning to sparkle again. A few tipsy tourists had burst into song, I didn't feel quite so forlorn any more. I took Mama's arm, we would join the crowd, we'd go and see the river, plop ourselves down in some bar and have a steaming-hot toddy. How about the bar where I'd worked for a couple of summers when I was at university? Mama brightened up, I became her child again.

Now she was dipping into old memories. I made comments, travelling across the years. I'd add a missing detail, the garish blue colour of my dress, a botched haircut, and that Dutch lover whose blond, athletic form suddenly came back to life even though I hadn't thought of him in years. I'd been so unhappy when he'd had to return to his country. Surely he was married, and had children. Or was divorced, why not? One out of every two marriages these days. I could have met him in Tunis, and everything might have started up again. Alessandro would have slipped past me like a shadow, I wouldn't have noticed. It takes so little for a person's life to veer in one direction or another. I looked at my watch. In Carthage, daybreak was near. Were you trying to find me in your sleep, Alessandro, while I strolled along with a woman who was terrified of you? *You have always liked foreigners.* I didn't respond. I kept walking on the snowy ground, glancing back every so often at the long trail of my footprints.

5

A clock inside my skull. I woke up this morning with a huge, well-oiled clock in my head. I'm going around in a circle, I'm gathering faces shattered by time. Anna, Mama, and France, Fanny's aunt, since suicides have first names, too. And I'm afraid for Fanny, afraid for myself. No woman around us can hold out a helping hand. We have to learn to cope on our own. Fanny laughs through her tears, I'm being stupid again, how she wishes she were an orphan, she would be able to enroll quietly in literature courses. Or film studies, like Étienne. He is lucky, his mother approves, Vincent and Emma support him too. With a gleam in her eye she adds, *Can you see me studying business administration?* Both of us giggle. What planet do mothers really live on?

Mama hadn't mentioned Alessandro again in Quebec City. You would think he no longer existed. But just as I was about to close up my suitcase, she blurted out once more, *Please be very careful, Anne.* I replied, *You too, Mama,* as though I hadn't understood. Then the taxi turned into our street. I stepped outside, it was the same large grey car as the last time. A knowing wink from the driver, *The bus station?* I nodded as I waved goodbye to Mama. In a little over three hours I would be home, there would be a message from

Alessandro. I would fire back a letter I had already composed in my head, it would end with one of the Italian phrases I knew, *Ti amo*, or *Ti penso con tutto l'amore che sai*. I wasn't going to be careful, Mama. People can't always live under a bell jar. And yet ... The moment I sat down before the screen, all the phrases in my letter vanished into thin air, the only thing that came into my mind was a plea, how did you go about leaving, Alessandro?

We'll find a solution, Fanny. I articulate each syllable as in an elocution class. Who is Fanny's mother? I have seen her photograph, an elegant woman, a calm smile, totally unlike her sister's smile as she spread her arms in empty space. But who would have thought Anna was Papa's sister? And that Elsa is Alessandro's sister? I hardly know anything about her, we've barely mentioned her name a couple of times. She has always lived on the same street as her mother, looked after her until her last breath. *She* had always stayed close to Sofia.

Was your aunt really crazy, Fanny? I ask her this for the very first time. Fanny shrugs, she doesn't want to search for an answer. I won't find out anything more, I'll just have to keep mulling over the few remarks that have slipped out during our conversations. Comments that don't explain a thing. She liked books. The movies. And blue eyeshadow. She always went away to the seaside on holiday in the summer, with her husband. She had married for love. Her husband was a handsome man. He has moved out now, he's living with another woman. *Already, Fanny?* She took a drag on her cigarette, she said gloomily, *He has forgotten*.

6

It was going to be a beautiful Sunday. A generous sun swept across the room, I had just received a short message from Alessandro, this evening I would have dinner with Jean-Bernard. Then the telephone rang. *You don't know me.* A man's voice. He introduced himself right away. Gianni, Alessando's son. He was in New York on business, he was coming to Montreal, he wanted to meet me. I said, *Montreal is seven hours from New York.* He answered, *One hour by plane.* With a shaky voice I arranged to meet him at the office. I would take him to our restaurant, we were going to be on my own territory. I repeated, *Wednesday at five.* I had to hang up, because I was suddenly back in the bathtub, staring at my spider's corner on the ceiling. I kept hearing Mama's voice, *Please be very careful, Anne.* Perhaps mothers are able to sense danger ahead.

The whole city is having a leisurely stretch, strollers occupy the street, the faithful serenely trickle out of a church. They don't know that a woman is watching them, from high up, behind the window of an apartment building. Wednesday at five. Slowly I regain my composure and conjure up my battle plans. Will I be artless? Seductive? Cold? Will I speak bluntly? Tonight I'll spread my cards out on the table, Jean-Bernard will give me his opinion. He relishes this kind of predicament, he'll forget about his lover for a minute or two. We'll have a good belly laugh together. When love is threatened, people aren't very subtle or refined. They join the great sea of humanity, below its outer layer of culture, good manners, sophistication. They are reduced to their humblest selves.

Two old people walk by, holding hands. They could easily look ridiculous, but they don't. I can see Alessandro and me thirty years from now. Alessandro won't be stooped, he will still be handsome and in love with me. Together we will trot along on the streets of Montreal. Or Rome. Or Carthage.

I am anxious to stroll along the streets of Rome with you. I dissected this message while taking one of my scalding-hot baths. To write it, you must have envisioned us together at your place. The message reveals things you aren't saying, at least not yet, but it does tell me you picture us in Rome. I take heart. On Wednesday I will be gorgeous, sure of myself, and calm. I solemnly promise. Your son will be powerless against us. I'm a warrior, I'm going to defend us.

7

The ceiling light is mirrored in the glass of the Leonor Fini picture across from me, I just can't take my eyes off it. It looks like a crystal ball. I tried to read, a collection of poems Fanny left with me, but the lines bobbed up and down and everything became blurred — the letters, the images, the meaning of the words, the meaning of life. I've put the book back on my bedside table, I wait. Obviously, I won't be able to get any sleep at all. I peer into the ring of light in the glass of the Leonor Fini as though Gianni's intentions were about to emerge, suddenly as plain as day. I still don't know why he made the trip from New York to come and meet me. It was almost as if I weren't his father's lover last night. Merely an old acquaintance, the friend of a friend, a distant cousin one takes the trouble to visit, it will be a pleasant evening.

I have no real proof Gianni tried to seduce me, just a vague feeling, a hunch that I was dodging some trap. I elegantly draped my hand over my wineglass when he wanted to fill it up for the third time. *You're being very virtuous.* He flashed a stagey smile. Is he really a son of Alessandro's, of the man who spills ash on the carpet when he fills his old pipe? That suave gesture of Gianni's when he wanted to offer me a cigarette, the smooth movement of his hand, his subtle pout as he looked at the empty package, and then that smile again, he happened to have another package in his coat pocket. The women at the next table stole glances at him when he headed for the cloakroom, I couldn't help noticing. I kept watching the tall receding figure with Alessandro's words running through my mind, Gianni looks like his mother. Against my will, I had been drawn into Jasmina's mystery.

I proposed a toast to our first meeting while lightly skipping over the word *first*, I didn't want to twist the knife in the wound too much. We were going to see each other again, yes, there wasn't the slightest doubt about that. He smiled. Gianni was sharp, he'd understood. Almost immediately he shed his smile and inquired, *Tell me about yourself*. I did, but guardedly, I let work take up all the space between us, the routine tasks of an architect, and then, without realizing it, we crossed the Atlantic, we ended up on the great square in Florence with Leonardo and Michelangelo, painters he was in daily contact with at the museum. Then on to New York — he had come to organize a large exhibition, he was going to send me a special invitation, could I perhaps take time out to go to the preview? Softening towards him all of a sudden, I promised I'd be there. But now I was tossing aside my firm resolutions, I needed to pull myself together.

He made me blush when after a soulful silence he declared, *I can see why my father is in love with you*. I should have responded with some witticism or pointed out that I was in love as well. I kept silent, though, feeling utterly incapable of speech. I just sat there, being stupid the way women sometimes are in the presence of a ladies' man. I wasn't able to protect us, Alessandro. Did Gianni notice? He took his eyes off my face to watch the dark forms behind the window as they scurried past, trying to outpace the gathering darkness. I failed to protect us while you were asleep, suspecting nothing, your nostrils full of smells rising from earth scorched by centuries of sunshine.

This evening you'll tell me about your day with the students. Just as you used to tell Jasmina when you came home at night. It's Gianni who said so. All I did was utter the word *tomb* and your other life suddenly loomed up before me. Gianni knows how to tell a good story, in a simple way, with exactly the right amount of emotion at the most intense moments. I listened, uneasy, jealous. Yes, jealousy reared its head again when images from Tunis brought Jasmina back. But I stood up to the dead woman until the end, without flinching. I needed to get used to this as well — there would be times when memories of long ago superimposed themselves on reality. It could be Gianni, Marco, or even you, Alessandro. During a family gathering someone would recall a gesture among the vast number of gestures from earlier days, and I would sit there smiling inanely, because that gesture would shut me out. I was the outsider, the one who doesn't fully join in the party. I would try to catch the eye of Marco's wife, who hadn't known the blissful days in Tunis either. I would manage to get used to it. Glued to my chair, I'd wait for the present to reassert itself. Marco's son would knock against a piece of furniture, they'd comfort him, or it could be the telephone, or more food might need to be brought to the table. I would brush against your arm, Alessandro, to remind you of *my* body. You would quiver, you'd imagine my night smells, the living memory that was going to silence your other memory. The body always has the last word.

What will Gianni do today before his plane leaves? He'll probably sit around, waiting. He looked disappointed when the taxi stopped in front of the building here. For a fleeting moment I nearly invited him in for one last drink. I resisted, he wasn't going to set foot in our private place, Alessandro. He kept my hand in his for an instant and said while his eyes sought out mine, *I would prefer our meeting to remain between ourselves.* I promised it would. I felt guilty, but at least he wasn't going to come up. This time, I had been able to protect us.

8

One whiff of Mama's eau de toilette and I am back at Sunday Mass, or out for one of our car rides along the river with Anna, as childhood suddenly breaks through my present life. Mama must have crossed the bridge by now, she is driving quietly along the highway, listening to her own music. In two hours she'll return to her loneliness. There is nothing I can do to help. Except invite her once in a while, rekindle her enthusiasm for the theatre, which she and Papa lost at the same time. Or take her out for a meal. And listen to her talking about Anna — Anna loved watching television, she dreamed of being as slim again as she'd been at twenty, she could recite from memory a paragraph read moments ago in the newspaper. Already as a schoolgirl she must have been phenomenally intelligent, while Papa was quite happy being like any other little boy on this earth.

I found out nothing. We circled around Anna's mystery without making any progress. Anna's madness would be shut inside her urn for all eternity. Just as it would for Fanny's aunt. No sooner had the coffin been lowered into the grave than the family stopped asking questions. Even Fanny. I was there, I had taken her aunt's place, my arms had opened for her. Mama has no one left but me. But I never could throw open my arms to her. I expected questions about Alessandro, they didn't come. Perhaps Mama is no longer worried. I'm alone, he's far away, he doesn't pose a threat any more. It was only a passing fancy.

This morning, when I read your message, Alessandro, I simply melted. I would come home from work one evening to find you comfortably settled in the armchair again. Those were your very words. I hastily clicked *Close*, Mama was just getting up, another thing she wasn't going to know. I made the coffee, I stared at the ham and eggs in the frying pan as if it were a mirror where you might suddenly appear, Alessandro, in all your glorious craziness. Such a wild scheme — you'd probably come to your senses during the day and write, *I was only dreaming for a moment.* I was quietly dreaming, too. Mama, though, had become talkative again, what a delightful play, Papa would've loved it! He never went to the theatre any more, but I held my tongue, I would have spat out one of those nasty comments I'm so good at whenever Mama turns soft-hearted and forgiving. I was determined to make the happy mood last, to spread it over the entire surface of the day. I suggested we make a reservation straightaway for the next production. Mama didn't protest. So I picked up the calendar and dialled the theatre's number. Nobody there, of course. I left a message, it was done, the day started off pointing towards the future, I had managed to pull Mama over to the right side of life.

The joy I already felt as a tiny girl whenever I came home from school with an angel pasted beside my name on an arithmetic test. Later, time does its best to snatch us from the world of angels. Our mothers now remind us of women in novels who mourn the loss of a man. There is nothing we can do to comfort them. We will simply have to get used to it. And yet I feel a twinge in my stomach each time Mama says *Richard*, in the French way. Memories will always weigh heavily on the scales of time, there is nothing I can do. Except wander into your dream, Alessandro, spot you sitting in your chair. The caretaker has let you in, you've lit a fire, you're waiting for me. Your laugh is as broad as the ocean. Do we make love, or cook pasta? It doesn't matter, we are together, enveloped in the smell of burning logs and mellow lamplight. We are together, and that's enough.

9

Dazed, I stood still in the lobby for a moment. Fanny came walking towards me, with red lips and her aunt's radiant smile. I stammered out, *You look very beautiful tonight, Fanny*, and her perfect mouth widened all the way to her cheeks. Fortunately, Vincent arrived with Emma Villeray and Étienne's mother, Fanny went to join them. I managed to slip into the background, hoping the throbbing at my temples would calm down, while I kept repeating to myself, you're being superstitious, Anne Martin, a physical resemblance doesn't mean anything — are *you* like Anna? Why be so afraid for Fanny? In a few minutes the screening would begin, Fanny's everyday face would re-emerge and my fear melt away. I only needed to wait.

Now Étienne strode towards the front of the auditorium. With his tall silhouette outlined against the screen, he welcomed us in Jérôme's voice. I was taken aback. His mother, too, I'm sure, and Emma Villeray, unless they've both got used to these sudden apparitions. But is that possible? It must be. Just today, Marc alluded to one of Jérôme's famous temper tantrums at the office, and we all laughed, even Maria who never could stand his mood swings. We laughed heartily, with great affection, no one blamed him any longer, we'd forgiven him. I thought, it's not that we're being kind, we simply don't miss him any more. And yet, as Étienne explained the problems he'd encountered during the shooting, Jérôme's face grew clearer and clearer and, with it, a flood of images I was powerless to stop.

Fanny's body filled the rectangle of cloth. You saw her walking along with that light, springy step of hers, as if at any minute she was going to start skipping, then she slowed down, came to a complete stop, stood transfixed at the curb. Étienne approached with another girl, he passed right by Fanny without seeing her. And that other girl was actually Fanny as well, but this time with her aunt's red smile. My heart began to pound again. This was a scene they hadn't shown me. *There are some surprises, just you wait and see*, Fanny had said. Indeed there were, it had become a different film. Was the woman played by Fanny insane? Did Fanny suffer from a split personality? You couldn't tell. I felt tremendous fear, uncontrollable terror, it raced through all my nerves. Fanny had now disappeared from the picture. I huddled up against the back of my seat and waited. That honk, the screeching tires, the thud of a body colliding with metal, the screams of passersby. I dug my nails deep into the armrests. My heart was about to burst.

Scattered applause around me, echoed by more clapping throughout the theatre. When I opened my eyes, Fanny's name was on the screen. You could see her walking along slowly behind the other names as they rolled by. She wasn't dead, it would seem. But the thud droned on inside my head, the thud from Fanny's body roared in my ears. For me, the film ended there. I would reject any other interpretation. I was furious at Vincent who'd held the camera, furious at Étienne, at Fanny, and at all those people who were bringing down the house. I seethed with rage, a blind rage as overpowering as my fear. Why had Fanny agreed to be so frivolous about death? Why hadn't she warned me? Was it spitefulness or lack of concern?

I couldn't bring myself to go and congratulate Fanny. Her friends surrounded her, my absence would go unnoticed. Silently I listened to one of the teachers at the college complimenting Étienne on the script's open ending. I'd had enough, I was going home. Near the cloakroom, I passed Emma Villeray. She gazed at me with anxious eyes, it was unmistakable. I wasn't alone.

10

It's fiction. It's imaginary. I threw down my calculator and flashed Jean-Bernard one of my darkest looks. The words gushed from my mouth, a shower of needles, the words of a woman spewing up her bile. Jean-Bernard didn't flinch. Sitting back, his arms folded, he waited. I was bound to cool down in the end. But the words kept pouring out, I really was possessed. How far was that simple comment going to take me?

The day had got off to a bad start. I'd had my nightmare again, there was no message from Alessandro this morning, but one from Fanny, she wanted to try out her new e-mail. She asked if I'd enjoyed their film, everybody had loved it. My anger had resurfaced. And yet, dazzling sunlight streamed in through the window, spring was on its way. I could have chosen to believe in her innocence. She had told Étienne her aunt's story, they changed the script, I shouldn't search any further. She only needed to die on the screen, while I had seen her die in real life. That was all, why should I worry?

What made me blow up, I wonder? Jean-Bernard's tone of voice or his assurance? He hadn't even been able to come to the première — that talk he was giving at seven. Big tears started running down my cheeks, I cried until all my anger had drained away. The film script was certainly not based on an imaginary event, how could Jean-Bernard so confidently split it off from reality? My tears dried up, I was able to breathe more easily. I talked about Fanny's smile, so strangely similar to her aunt's, and the muffled thud at impact, the screams, and death entering every cell of my body. I talked about the real scene that Jean-Bernard never saw.

A sweet song now filtered into the room. The secretary had just arrived. Jean-Bernard went to meet her, closing my office door behind him. I reached for my bag. I took out my mirror, then the concealer stick, I would try to draw a face for myself. If all else failed, I would claim I'd had one of my sleepless nights. Marc would believe me, the contractor, too. But not Maria or Dominique, they would know. They knew when the pouches beneath one's eyes were lingering traces of a crying spell.

11

Patches of colour flit about on the watery whiteness. Green, blue, and black patches break up the monotony of the landscape, but my eyes are riveted to a tiny red dot as it fades into nothingness. Fanny suddenly leaned forward to gain momentum and whizzed down the hill. Jean-Bernard's familiar laugh rang out, and I burst out laughing, too. My anxiety has gone. Since I had a talk with Fanny, I no longer hear the dull sound from her body in the film. As she glides over the snow, she looks surprisingly graceful, you forget that her feet are wedged into skis, she's about to disappear below the horizon.

Jean-Bernard and I quietly follow one another on the trodden snow. We slip our feet into each other's tracks, we take the time to feel every stab of our poles into the ground, we let our minds roam. Some day I'll walk the Santiago de Compostela route. Jean-Bernard shouts out, *The route of the Milky Way!* He would like to do the pilgrimage with me. It's by Alessandro's side that I see myself striding along beneath the Spanish sun, but he has no idea. When two people aren't in love, how much closeness can they achieve?

Family rate, the parking attendant called out in a self-assured voice when the car stopped at the ticket booth. Despite my protests, Jean-Bernard pulled out his wallet. He was playing the game — the perfect father, perfect husband. A shiver ran down my back, everything would be so simple if we were together. How cruel desire is, cruel and mysterious. I glanced over at Jean-Bernard as he tried to find a parking spot while he discussed the course with Fanny. He knew the pitfalls of each trail — didn't he come here several times a week every winter to go cross-country skiing, when he lived near the mountain? On Sundays, Jérôme often joined him with Emma and Étienne. Too bad Étienne wasn't free today. *He's a good skier, Étienne. Jérôme, too*, he added, his voice cracking. Jean-Bernard's voice occasionally caught in his throat when he remembered Jérôme. It was something he had never dared bring up with me. Our closeness stopped short of that impassable boundary.

Only two kilometres to go, says the sign. We continue on, our minds a blank. *We should've brought along some water*. Jean-Bernard yells, *Next time*. Yes, there will be other beautiful Saturdays before spring returns, we'll come back with Fanny, and Étienne, just as when he was little, and perhaps also with Alessandro, if he gets to the stage of fusing his dreams with reality. A stocky man went past a short while ago, with a salt-and-pepper beard. Fanny pointed him out to me with her ski pole. Yes, I'd noticed him, I jump whenever I see someone who looks like Alessandro.

The black roof at the bottom of the hill is growing larger. We're almost there, only a few more minutes of trudging ahead of us. Our muscles move slowly, they feel heavier and heavier. Fanny is sure to make fun of us, *You finally made it!* And I'll be able to take part in the teasing, delighted by her arrogance. Jean-Bernard gets ready to race down the slope, and I watch him, his supple form, graceful as that of a twenty-year-old. He presses down on his skis, lets himself be carried along, succeeds in keeping his balance. One last curve and he comes to a halt right beside the man with the salt-and-pepper beard. Yet he doesn't seem to notice the resemblance. He calls out to me instead, but I look at the slope and I'm afraid, suddenly I'm afraid to ski down, afraid I won't be able to stop, afraid of the dull sound of my body hitting against one of those big trees at the bottom, afraid of being killed beside that man who looks like you, Alessandro, and next to Fanny. There she is coming out of the snack bar with her funny red tuque pulled down over her forehead. She runs towards Jean-Bernard, she points at me while I bend over to undo the clasp on my skies.

They are having a good laugh at my expense down below. They say to each other, *Some day, Anne will have to learn to handle the simple things of life.* Skiing down a slope, knowing how to look after a cat, learning to drive a car, daring to watch, with eyes wide open, someone being killed on the screen. But perhaps, like some old medal, my fear will always dangle from my neck, I will need to walk down ski slopes, planting my feet solidly into the snow. Is that really so terrible? I am breathing, I cook meals, and I'm learning to love a man who looks just like the one I'm plodding towards right now, my eyes squinting into the late-winter sun. This isn't the right moment to die, I know when to be careful. All it takes, sometimes, is the smallest thing, a gesture, a glance, a crazy image slipping over the picture of happiness. It takes so little to fling us into the timeless void.

12

Everything is there. The tuques and scarves on the carpet by the door, the bottle of wine on the table, your Phoenician statuettes, the logs in the hearth. Jean-Bernard lights the fire, and Fanny reads us her latest poem. All is well with the world, the blood in my veins flows at the proper speed again. The body forgets fear much faster than we do. A minute ago, Fanny looked up from her sheet of paper and said, *We'll teach her to ski down a slope yet.* Jean-Bernard replied, *I've given up.* Fanny didn't respond. Knitting her brow, she crossed out a line. Jean-Bernard winked at me. *Giving up* were words Jean-Bernard and I would share between the two of us. I've noticed a new wrinkle furrowing Jean-Bernard's lip, a wrinkle etched by sorrow. His last lover, most likely. What a pity life teaches us to give up. A love, a ski slope — perhaps it's the same fear. One sees a hollow skull looming in the distance, it stares at us from empty sockets, and without a moment's thought we say no. We won't go any further. We grow accustomed to going round and round on life's circular path.

Now Jean-Bernard laughs, his face bent over Fanny. *Such a cliché she's just written!* She raises her head towards me, but I can't defend her, she's well aware of that, it's Jean-Bernard who knows about poetry. Another stroke through the word she'd found. Her forehead creases again, she searches, then abruptly puts the sheet of paper down on the table, she'll solve it tomorrow. Not even a hint of doubt in her voice. Jean-Bernard stares at her in amazement, as though he were suddenly looking at an old picture of himself. He smiles. Exuding self-confidence, Fanny is beautiful.

She has now stretched out on the carpet in front of the fire. With drowsy eyes she tries to read the flames. Gently she surrenders to sleep, she knows I'll make up a lemon-scented bed for her in a little while, just as her Aunt France used to do, when death was no more than a hazy notion in her mind, something that happened only to the elderly and the sick. Did people throw themselves off the rocks at Carthage, Alessandro? I've never thought of asking you.

Fanny is now sound asleep. Jean-Bernard yawns, stands up, says, *I'm off.* I tell him he can stay over if he wants to, but he doesn't accept, you can't go on crying for ever and ever, world without end, amen. Especially if you sense the horizon getting closer and closer. A strange feeling comes over me, a malaise that grips my jaws. I just can't shake it off, I imagine the words *giving up* in Alessandro's mouth. I try to cling to his love letters, they're right there, inside a mauve folder in my filing cabinet, I'll only have to reread them in a minute or two, when Jean-Bernard will have walked out the door.

But Jean-Bernard sits down again, pours himself another glass of wine, he looks wide awake now. He asks, *Did I upset you?* I pour myself a glass, too. I talk about weariness making a muddle of phrases and faces, the tiring effect of all that fresh air and the wine. Even at my age, even though I know full well

I won't die of a broken heart any more, there's something very sad about the thought that one day Alessandro and I might be nothing but old friends. Jean-Bernard mulls it over, his eyes fixed on the dying flames. He states that I have nothing to fear from Alessandro, he is a man who has loved a woman until her dying day. He adds, *One just knows, Anne.* Jean-Bernard's positive tone. Did he know, about Jérôme, what Judith and Emma hadn't known? Did Mama know about Papa? But I won't ask anything else. Not tonight.

13

I've tidied up, dusted, vacuumed. The apartment could be used as the setting for one of those commercials for miracle cleaning products that interrupt women's television programmes. Everything irritated me when I got up this morning. The cigarette smell embedded in the clothes, the stale wine at the bottom of the glasses, the grumpy look on Fanny's face, and the memory of the word *decision*. *Decision*, I had woken up with just that one word in my head, it would be fused to my brain for the rest of the day. I know myself by now. Fanny's eyelids gradually came unstuck, she started to talk. I listened, trying to fight off a mounting uneasiness. I hadn't made myself clear last night, Jean-Bernard had left without understanding my reasons. As he slipped on his coat, he'd said, *You and Alessandro will need to make a decision one of these days.* What decision? But Jean-Bernard hadn't let go, he'd kept urging me in that steady tone of his, the one that forces municipal government officials and contractors to revise their calculations. He'd made a good case, but I wouldn't play his game, I'd refused the word *decision* to the very end.

Suddenly Fanny said, *There's something bothering you.* I tried to cover up but it all tumbled out, I told her everything. Everything. Oh well, never mind. I'm not a mother, duty bound to screen information for her children. She went to get another cigarette, she really was smoking like a chimney in January. I made no comment, though. I had to be consistent — did I want to play the mother or not? I waited for her to light up, she was going to say, *You're being stupid*, I would start laughing. But she took long drags on her cigarette, oblivious to the awkward silence. Finally, she stubbed out the butt in the ashtray and confessed, *I don't want you to leave.*

My uneasiness grew. I was blaming myself. I ought to reassure Fanny, explain that I wasn't going to leave. She could count on me. So could Mama, and Jean-Bernard, and the others at the office. Then it dawned on me that perhaps this was all Jean-Bernard was hoping for — to hear me calmly say, *I'm not leaving*. The furrow disappeared from Fanny's brow. The air in the room began to feel soft and light again. I got up to open the window, I would spend the afternoon putting the apartment in order. It looked like a wasteland. I turned down Fanny's offer to help, I needed to be alone.

I cleaned, but it wasn't enough. I spotted the chaos in the wardrobes. The summer clothes hadn't been stowed away in their usual boxes, that is where Fanny's aunt had led me. I slid back into my old gestures, the ones Mama had never forsaken, not even in the fall after Papa left. Mama was strong. I placed the clothes on the bed, divided my life into two separate piles, summer and winter. The sun would be here in a few short weeks, but it didn't matter, I would simply unpack my boxes, start all over again. Then I decided to throw out Anna's things, the ones Mama had brought me. I wasn't going to be saddled with them any longer.

A thick woollen cardigan, a string of pearls, a dressing gown, I spread everything out in front of me on the sofa in the living room. Beautiful things. One can be insane and still have good taste. I sat down and took a good look. The cardigan, I would be able to wear. The pearls, too, and also the dressing gown, when mine was dirty. You don't catch madness the way you catch a bad cold. All I would have to do was slip them on, all I would need to do was wait till they took on the smell of my own skin.

Part V

1

First the sky grew dim, then the river, then the moored form that seemed to have forgotten the very notion of the sea. It all merged into various shades of a thin, dismal grey. Evening was closing in, while I scanned the fading lines and angles, not quite ready yet to reach for the lamp switch. The hour when melancholy strikes. Soon the city would light up like a fairground, the office would empty. I just had to be patient for a moment. Before long, there would be peace and quiet. Just be patient, yes, that's what I needed to tell myself again while I picked up the phone. Probably someone from the permit office, more explaining to be done. With a hint of irritation in my voice I articulated, *Anne Martin*. A booming laugh instantly enveloped me. I gripped the receiver as if it could vanish into thin air. Alessandro's voice seemed real, though, when he told me he was over at my place, sitting in his chair. I hung up with the words *I'm waiting for you* in my head. The new secretary's face dropped when I shouted on my way out, *An emergency*. I made an effort to regain my composure, I said, *A client who's going off on a trip tomorrow*. Her features went back to normal, she was almost reassured.

The elevator wouldn't come. The taxi stopped at every traffic light, it was rush hour, why hadn't I taken the subway?

My building at last. I paid without waiting for the change, in minutes I would be opening the door of my apartment. I got out my lipstick in the lobby and gave myself lips like those of the woman who hovered over the museum. I was ready.

He was dozing in the armchair. I gently slipped the pipe out of his fingers and planted a kiss on his cheek. I ended up locked in his arms, submerged in the smell of earth, jasmine, and tobacco all in one, the smell of Alessandro Moretti. I stayed there, not worrying if I'd be able to move, get up, cook dinner, go back to work the next day, send documents to the permit office for the umpteenth time. We sat there bonded to one another until the sombre darkness swallowed us up. Then that gurgling in Alessandro's stomach. Again, I heard his deep, hearty laugh. We had to accept that once more we would be two separate bodies. Alessandro said, *I'm going to light a fire,* and this ordinary phrase rekindled the tenderness surrounding those simple gestures we'd grown used to making together. I tore myself away from his scent to go and cook pasta. I asked, *Pesto? Tomato sauce?* in the same tone of voice as when I asked a client, *Would you prefer to have the bathroom on the right-hand side of the hallway or the left-hand side?* We had moved back into our own flow, a prosaic, unheroic one.

It hadn't occurred to us to make love. For a second I wondered if we still felt desire for each other but, while reaching for the refrigerator door, Alessandro placed his hand on the nape of my neck, and I quivered. Desire was alive. Alessandro took out the bottle of olive oil, and I tore open the pasta package. In a little while we would become one flesh again, but first we would share every single particle of space. I thought of animals establishing their territory. I thought, we will be husband and wife once again, we'll make love like a couple, how do couples make love?

You seem awfully pensive. Alessandro handed me a glass of wine and I smiled at him. Not even a hint of worry in his eyes, he quietly let his life unfold, he hadn't discovered anything new about the Phoenicians, but he was confident. *I'm searching,* he said. *One must never stop searching.* The water for the pasta was beginning to bubble, a woman's smile floated on the surface, at what point had Fanny's aunt given up telling herself, *One must never stop searching?* But now Alessandro lifted up my sweater, caressed my breasts. I heard words I didn't understand, they were words of love, those are words one just knows.

2

It's not so much grief as a last shred of hope she has never been able to relinquish. One day, her life would slip back into its familiar pattern, predictable as the circular sweep of the hands of a clock. One day, Papa might realize he hadn't forgotten. I've only now understood. I had thought of changing our reservation for the theatre, but Alessandro objected. Sooner or later he would have to meet my mother, wouldn't he? I gave in. On the telephone, there was a tiny pause when I let her know, then the suggestion I had been expecting, why deny myself the pleasure of going to the performance with Alessandro? I answered back, I really wanted to see it with *her*. She agreed — curiosity, motherly concern — all right, she would come. She was going to stay at a hotel, though.

She arrived at my place just before dusk. Such uneasiness, already, when I introduced Alessandro to her, a malaise bringing back smells of incense and lilacs, crinolines, the proprieties, my whole childhood. Alessandro didn't have Papa's polished manners. Nor his strong presence. He wasn't the kind of man Mama would have chosen. Then he laughed his stentorian laugh while telling us about his excavations at Carthage, and little by little Mama's world fell apart. It was beyond her wildest dreams that her daughter's lover might have spent all of his life digging the ground of a country that didn't belong to us. In the theatre, before the curtain went up, she would say, *He is nice.* I had heard her use that phrase dozens of times. Even about Eileen. She would list the good qualities, you'd have to guess the bad ones.

Alessandro will never be able to forget. This comment I hadn't anticipated. I felt dizzy all of a sudden, the stage began to bob up and down. Fortunately the lights were flashing, in a few minutes it would be dark, I could confront the darkness within me. Now the actresses appeared before us one by one, mourning their dead daughters, but I didn't believe in it. All I could see was my own mother looming like a tree with enormous roots, a behemoth planted at the very centre of the Earth, sheltering in its foliage the living image of Jasmina. There she was, smiling and beautiful, her beloved son clinging to her knees. Why did Mama lure her back tonight, just when she no longer haunted me? I very nearly stood up and shouted, *It's Gianni who will mourn Jasmina for all eternity, not Alessandro.* I had almost managed to calm down when the first ripple of applause rang out. The performance was over. I was going to take Mama back to her hotel, we would have a drink at the bar, discuss the play's mothers and daughters. We had always talked much more easily about the theatre than about real life.

It was close to midnight when I got home. Alessandro wasn't asleep. He was waiting for me in his armchair. He put a yellow book down on the little table, next to his pipe. He wanted me to tell him about the evening, but right away the image of Gianni on Jasmina's knees leapt into my mind, and of Mama, and all the mothers from the play. How many of them would start to live again after the grieving? Stupidly, I let Mama's comment at the theatre slip out, I just couldn't keep it to myself any longer. Alessandro slowly filled his pipe and lit it. Then he spoke. *Perhaps I should have lain down on a funeral pyre.* My eyes blurred with tears. He picked up the yellow book from the little table and read out, *Love gets us through the days, helps us through the nights. / Love destroys the old and ushers in the new.* I pleaded, *Say it again.* But all he did was hand me the book. *Poets say it so much better than I could.*

3

Have you called Toronto? Jean-Bernard leans against the door-post. I nod my head, *Nobody home.* I'm lying. What an idea to have suggested hiring Michael as a trainee this summer — I really don't know what came over me. Perhaps I wanted to steal Eileen's son away from her, revenge is sweet. Or else it's this spring sun, a sky without ghosts, a peaceful sky today, belonging only to the living. And Alessandro, of course, aren't I a woman in love? Jean-Bernard insists, *We need someone.* Again, I nod. I'm not going to tell him I'm wavering, I have no desire to sort out my feelings. I look up the number I've never been able to memorize and hold my breath while pressing the keys. Papa's voice on the answering machine, I won't have to talk to him, neither him nor Eileen. I leave a few bunched-up sentences, a compact unit impossible to break. Now all I have to do is wait. They're sure to call me back.

Last night, Alessandro handed me a photograph he'd found inside one of my old design journals. Papa with Anna. I heard, *He's a good-looking man.* My eyes bored into Papa's face so I might see him smile on Anna's arm. I had taken the photo myself, on a summer Sunday like any other — roses in the gar-den, Anna's gaudy, flowered dress, a cold meal about to be laid out under the willow tree. That man with the smile is my father, that woman his sister. She doesn't look like a madwoman, her eyes fastened on her brother's smile while Mama spreads out the red-and-white chequered tablecloth. You never see Mama on our Sunday photographs. Papa and Anna are huddled up together in a single childhood — who could tell then that Papa was going to leave one day, that Sundays wouldn't be the same any more? There's no date on the photograph. Were Eileen and Papa lovers that summer? That's another thing I'll never know.

What *does* one ever know? Alessandro took refuge in his armchair. He began to draw on his pipe, pensive, or nostalgic, like a man who suddenly gives up searching. A snapping sound came from the fireplace. We needed to add another log, perform gestures that deliver their own answers. I decided to lay the photo down on the table beside the Phoenician gods, those deities who demanded that people kill children in order to be saved. I said, *We don't have a single photo of us, Alessandro.* But he shrugged his shoulders, gleefully poked the smoldering wood, we didn't need any photographs since we were going to be together for the rest of our lives. He said that as if it were self-evident.

4

Am I going or not? Confusion in my mind again, my brain is all stirred up, I'm unable to make a decision. What I need is an oracle. In the newspaper this morning I fell upon the horoscopes. It predicted stability for me, so I closed it up again with a laugh. Serves me right for being such a foolish woman. For the umpteenth time I reread the form, as though the future might suddenly burst forth from the shadow of the words. No hidden signs, however. Just these tiny, rigid, black characters, recalling the competition's rules and the voice of the female official on the telephone, the Prix de Rome, yes. A year in Rome, a studio apartment, a grant.

Nearby, Alessandro's slow breathing, a man asleep. I turned the same thoughts over and over in my mind between the sheets until I became deeply distressed, then I got up, I wouldn't be able to go back to sleep. There are no calculations that can silence anguish. It clings to our cells, paralyses us, the heart thuds inside an iron cage. I sit and wait, the damp sheets of paper between my sticky hands, I am trying to find a project. I arrived home this evening with that vertical crease between my eyebrows, Alessandro asked me what was the matter. I didn't say anything about the Prix de Rome. I simply said there were problems on the building site. An easy answer —

not a day goes by without problems for an architect. I would talk to him when my decision was made. He didn't press me. Then his face lit up, Michael had left a message, he was thrilled about that training course, he would come to meet Jean-Bernard and me as soon as we'd like.

You're not sleeping? Alessandro is looking at me, his eyelids stuck together, his hair all tousled. He isn't the brilliant archaeologist of Carthage, but a man who looks like any other sleepy human. Vulnerable. He plops himself down beside me on the sofa, takes the sheets of paper in his hands, squints at them, but the tiny characters dance in front of his far-sighted eyes, he passes me the form, what is it? I don't hold back any longer, I explain. In the silence of the night everything is so much easier. I think out loud, the Prix de Rome, a year in Rome for an architectural project, do I apply for it or not?

Now Alessandro is wide awake. He hunts for his pipe, puts on his glasses, wraps his arm around my shoulders. But a blank face looms up behind the lamp, and my mind becomes muddled. I'm afraid, so afraid, everything goes dark within me. Whose face is it? I don't know. It's simply there, outlined against the grey lace of the lamp. It watches me. Love isn't a wonderland with genies and princes, it confronts an expressionless face in the lace of a lamp, which I can't take my eyes off.

Alessandro went to get some paper. Now he picks up his pen from the table, beside the Phoenician gods, and starts to talk. I could study the Etruscan necropolises near Rome. Rome takes shape beneath his hand, with its conquests and monuments. Gradually it loses its battles, falls into decay, then it's rebuilt through the brambles and ruins. This is the

Rome I love, the city that rises continually from its ashes. Alessandro strolls along a street reserved for pedestrians, he climbs up the squat tower of the castel Sant'Angelo, lingers on the piazza Navona, does the shopping with Gianni. He goes to a lecture, gives his first kiss to the little girl next door, walks his younger sister to school, runs in the park with his cousins from Pescara. He watches the soldiers going up to see his mother, he hears her shrieking the name of his father who won't be coming back.

The sky lights up the window and little by little the face becomes blurred. All that remains is an oval, growing longer and longer before daylight swallows it up. Time to go to work soon. I haven't slept a wink as yet, I must try to get some sleep. I follow Alessandro into the bedroom, feeling peaceful now, as when we make our way towards ancient ruins that no longer remember humanity's mistakes.

5

Once again, on top of the museum, those brilliantly red lips, soaring into the sky. The woman has taken up winter's bet — the wind, the snow — she is still here, looking confident in the March light. *She's a believer*, says Alessandro. Fanny stares at him in wide-eyed amazement, how can one tell? He shrugs, confidence is something you recognize. Fanny gazes up again, searches, asks me if I see it. I don't know what to answer — the woman is there, totally present in her lips suspended in mid-air, but who knows when a violent gust of wind is going to bring her down? The impact of her skull, the shattered lips. I don't say it, though. Not in this bluish light, not in front of Fanny.

She glows with happiness today, she has applied for entrance into a literature programme, her mother gave in because of her poems, the ones that will be published in a magazine. She arrived at the door out of breath, just as we were putting on our coats. *Pilgrimage to the museum*, said Alessandro. *What's a pilgrimage?* Alessandro burst out laughing. He described the interminable journey with the sun beating down, the tiredness, the blisters on your feet — all those journeys human beings have undertaken to find a little peace. Some day he was going to bring us to Santiago de Compostela.

Fanny clapped her hands, she wanted to believe him. At that moment, I'm sure, she really did.

The lips seem to be moving. Alessandro, mesmerized, can't take his eyes off them, while I remain engrossed in my tiny life. But, even so, I manage to hold up my head. Yesterday, I dropped off my project at the post office. I will have that year in Rome, Alessandro doesn't doubt it for a minute. A wonderful project, closer to my heart than any other has been in a long, long while. It came to me the other night. Alessandro was talking about his wanderings through the streets of Rome. So many old stones and pillars he happens upon that have been incorporated into other buildings over the centuries, shamelessly, without a second thought, when history wasn't weighty enough yet to immobilize the present. This is what I would like to study, the integration of ancient ruins into the hustle and bustle of everyday life. I'm not interested in necropolises. I pulled out the books I have on Rome, we scribbled page after page, until we got the eras and the styles, the popes and emperors thoroughly mixed up. Then we crawled into bed, I hadn't been this happy in ages.

Alessandro and Fanny are chattering away as they head for the museum doors while I silently follow them. My fear has sneaked up on me again, as it does every time I think of the word *departure*. But I keep walking, I am able to take off my coat, say thank you when I'm handed my ticket, look at the paintings which hang close together in straight rows along the walls. You aren't locked inside your private world, Anne Martin. You can smile. At every step, you reconstitute an image of yourself that mirrors the one already present in people's minds. You aren't Anna. Nor Fanny's aunt. But is there a way of knowing if our life will veer out of control some day? Are there clearer signs than dizziness? A spell of weariness, ghosts staring at us, grinning maliciously?

Alessandro turned towards me before leading Fanny off to the adjoining gallery. I would catch up with them in a moment. Just being alone in here, having a long look, I may find myself again. Perhaps some madwoman has painted her pictures in the colour of humanity's unfathomable dread. Everything here is restrained, though. The paint is quite dry, it no longer suggests any sweat, or dirt, or smears on the fingers that hold the brush. I'm reminded of the plans I draw so relentlessly day after day. Not a single painting has been made with injured hands.

But Fanny comes rushing back, she grabs me by the sleeve, pulls me along. She takes me over to a painting. I stand transfixed. The fleecy white clouds. The greyish white building at the back. And that black form throwing herself out of the window, that form whose downward plunge we follow and who ends up on the ground, with her eyes open, lying in a pool of blood. So beautiful is she in death, it sends a deep shiver up my spine. The woman has a real name, Dorothy Hale, Fanny reads it out loud, and a real story, she threw herself out of the building on October 21, 1938, it's written down right there on the painting, but they don't tell us why, perhaps they don't know. My legs go wobbly, my whole body is limp, I remove my thick sweater, my eyes riveted all the while on the woman's face, it's as if Fanny's aunt were showing us her death. Fanny chatters on and on, then she touches me with an icy hand, so I fold her plump hands into my own. Just one thought comes into my head — don't you ever do that, Fanny, don't ever do that. But I clench my teeth so the words will dissolve inside my mouth.

Alessandro tenderly nudges us along, *I'm buying you a drink*. We place our feet into his footsteps, we follow him the way one follows the right road. Instinctively we trail him until behind us the museum closes on the eyes of Dorothy Hale, lying in her blood. Sunshine lights up the city, the red lips seem to smile almost indecently. Alessandro gets us to raise our heads, *she* is the woman we should look at. Without a word, he fills his pipe. Then he says dreamily, *The Milky Way. That's what the illuminated panel is called.*

6

Now sunlight is streaming down, and the airplanes spread their wings on the runway, they aren't afraid to fly across the seas. In the distance, the big-bodied jet Alessandro has boarded. Slowly it taxies away, slips beyond the window frame, soon it will be taking off. I cross my fingers — please let him arrive safe and sound. Thoughts of disaster crowd into my mind, that's part of being in love, it can't be helped. One blurts out stupid phrases, *Will you be careful?* Alessandro laughed, yet again. He promised he'd be careful, he wouldn't endanger his life just when I was about to settle in Rome. But what did we really know about it? We needed to wait, I wouldn't hear about the prize until May.

The plane has disappeared on the left behind the wall. Now the window only frames an empty space, busy maintenance people making empty gestures, and hulking empty jets. Back home, an empty bedroom. I don't want to go there. Fortunately there's the bar, humming with excitement at this time of day when there are so many departures. Not one table left, I have to sit at the bar. Wait till I'm spotted by the bartender, she is rushed off her feet. I'll wait here in the harsh light, all afternoon, all night. Beside me, a man who is going grey at the temples. I hadn't noticed him. Distinguished, like Papa. He breaks the ice,

In here, we are nowhere. He is right, the place looks like a theatre set. I reply, *Isn't that what we're looking for?* He stares at me in surprise. Then some words in his harsh language, and right away he apologizes, he translates, three more hours of waiting, his plane has been delayed, how about having a bite to eat together at the restaurant? Without a moment's hesitation, I follow him. I don't want to be alone either.

He lets out a great sigh as he sits down. Nervous laughter rises from my throat — all the emotions of the day, and also shame. No matter how often I remind myself that there's no harm in what I'm doing, it's always possible that one might weaken. Somebody's lip may curl in a certain way at just the right moment and we are affected in spite of ourselves, something has begun. There are times when we make love simply because we're bored. So many memories I would never reveal to Alessandro. A setting like this one, a mellow voice lulling me in a strange language, what year was it again? I had caught *Montreal*, I'd pricked up my ears, a wait of at least six hours. I could have wept. At the next table a man had burst out laughing, we'd looked at each other, exchanged a few words. Sometimes laughter is all it takes for two people to make contact. Then, in each other's company, we will string the minutes together until they form a smooth sequence. A pink necklace, like a string of candies. The wine has a nameless taste. The meal, too. But we can survive, we're surviving, five more hours to kill, who is waiting for me anyway? The man speaks the words I let him speak. I say yes while I swallow the last mouthful. We slip away from this nowhere meal, up to a nowhere room.

Tonight, however, we will quietly finish our escalopes. I will watch my gestures, I won't let the man sitting opposite me utter a phrase I don't want to hear. He talks, while I try to steer my gaze inward so I can see Alessandro's face again. I want to picture him flying calmly over the ocean, yes, he's flying along peacefully, I can relax, he won't fall from the sky. Our filled wine glasses clink brightly when they touch, the plates will arrive soon, we'll chat over our meal, then I'll be on my way again, alone. I'll return to my empty bedroom.

7

I'm going to leave. That's all I think about. In the morning, in front of the mirror, when I'm searching for my face, then before a huge subway poster that entices the mind into dreams of travel. I try to get used to the idea so it will become a statement. A statement I will be able to make quite calmly, articulating every word. Or I could leave a sheet of paper in the middle of the table. When it was found, I'd already be immersed in the street noises of Rome. I would have avoided the endless questions. And the tears. Fanny, Mama. Mama in particular. Mama's silence. No screams, no reproaches, only the trembling that will unnerve me, start me trembling as well. I will need to hold on to the words as if they were a wooden doorpost, a wall, an armchair to lean against. I will need to be able to breathe in and breathe out, move my lips, explain, act as though no misfortune or disaster had ever happened in our midst. I'll have to say I'm not crazy, I'm only going away for a year, isn't that what I used to do when I was a university student? Besides, Alessandro is right there, he has just had the apartment redecorated, we'll sleep in Marco's room, he's going to buy a brand new bed, in which he has never made love with Jasmina.

Gianni didn't flinch, so it seems, when he saw the work that was being done. He probably contemplated his cigarette smoldering between his fingertips, then stubbed it out abruptly in the ashtray. I'm sure he went on talking, his body supple and straight, about his projects, his work in Florence, the exhibition in New York. Last night, I woke up in a sweat, my temples throbbing wildly, I was sitting at a table with Gianni, I was trying to talk to him, and the features of Eileen's face gradually replaced my own. Gianni's eyes were silent, mute with dread, rage, horror — my words were deadly blows, finishing off his mother. Will he forgive me one day?

Mama's silence. It may finally get me to shout out, *Say something!* Or I'll ask her to grab my shoulders, give me a good shake, the way she'd shake out my thick duvet on the balcony. Surely, there must have been shouts, tears, insults, slaps between her and Papa, it's impossible to hear, *I'm leaving*, without this wrenching inside one's chest. Or else I'll shake *her*, I'll get her to admit once and for all, about the ripping sound in the chest, the wrenching. I'll force her to say that one can never forgive. Yet I know I won't say anything, I'll close my eyes, I'll think of you, Alessandro. I'll simply try not to fall apart.

8

Whatever possessed me, Anne Martin, to go and move in with a man I hardly knew, without having the slightest idea if I'd be awarded the Prix de Rome? I must have taken leave of my senses. My hand tightened around the cold glass. It felt disconnected from my body, metallic, a spanner, yes, I thought of a spanner. I should unclench my fingers, put my beer down on the table, say something. But I just sat there, motionless. Stupid. Uncompromising Dominique kept staring at an invisible spot behind me. I knew my colleague well, she wouldn't apologize. It was up to me to justify myself, I could do it, I'd always been able to defend my projects. This time, however, it concerned *me*. She had sunk her arrow into the very centre of the target.

There was no more talk about the architectural exhibition, the spell had been broken. Jean-Bernard held out his package of cigarettes to Marc, and Marc reached for it although he never smokes. A deep, heavy silence hanging over us, a November-like fog. We were all suddenly alone around the table, cut off from one another, as one sometimes is in a bar. Then a singer's voice washed over the silence, *Your love has changed my life*, and we burst out laughing, fits of nervous laughter, we remembered, the singer's name, the ridiculous lyrics, how old were we? I tried to come up with some retort that would floor Dominique, one of those blunt punches, but I could only think of complicated answers, wasn't love every bit as ridiculous in poetry as it was in trashy songs? Too bad then, I would look like all those naïve women blindly following a man, I would be judged, but did I really have to stay entombed in my image all my life?

The conversation started up again, Marc and Maria discussed the current building site, what else could we talk about? Jean-Bernard touched me lightly on my shoulder as though he were an angel straight from the pages of the little catechism book who chased away bad dreams. You would sleep soundly. I was going to miss Jean-Bernard, only him, along with Fanny. Yes. Mama, Jean-Bernard, and Fanny. Fanny had barely twitched when I finally decided to tell her. She'd lifted her fork to her mouth as if I hadn't said anything. At the far end of the restaurant a woman discreetly dried her eyes, the man sitting opposite her may also just have told her he was leaving. I thought of Mama. There had been no need for Papa to search for the right words, the situation had resolved itself, as if by magic. Luck had always been on his side. And what about Jérôme, what had he said to Emma Villeray? I pushed my plate away, the broccoli wasn't going to go down.

Fanny took forever to finish her meal, the food seemed to be regenerating on her plate with every mouthful, and all the while I fought against the silence. My voice remained stuck in my throat. But I did manage to utter, *I'm being stupid, really really stupid*, and the uneasiness faded. Now there was anger, how crazy to get oneself into such a state! I explained to Fanny that I expected her at my place in Rome for Christmas, I would help out, I was anxious to have her come and stay, so was Alessandro. At my place in Rome. For a brief moment the words sailed in space, like fragile birthday balloons. I added windows with curtains, some plants in a freshly painted living room, a cosy bed, the commonplace images of a commonplace kind of happiness. Of course, I had to skip over the gloomy things — Gianni might never accept me, Alessandro would keep getting older. I would end up alone one day, just like Mama, but I would cope. Hadn't I always?

Outside, the sun had melted the last patches of snow on the grassy borders, it still looked mild out, I finished my beer and decided to go home. I walked on, pushing Dominique's words into a tiny corner of my mind where they were powerless to interfere with the images I had constructed so patiently with Fanny. We're doing our shopping together in Rome. With Alessandro we visit the churches, squares, fountains, monuments, castles. We're taking the train to Florence. Fanny smiles, we aren't going to lose each other. Every day, she will send me messages. Life is offering more possibilities than before. And there will also be Étienne, and Jean-Bernard, and her mother, come to think of it. Sometimes mothers end up understanding, if we take the trouble to talk to them. I am trying to convince myself — I don't want to tell her that *I* never could.

9

No sooner did I glimpse his tall figure than bang! something raced through my skin, I stepped forward and threw open my arms to him. No reasoning can possibly account for that. For a moment my body was simply porous, unguarded. I should have apologized for being late, an emergency at the site. Instead, I sat down sideways to watch the proceedings. Jean-Bernard was explaining the work and Michael smiled in agreement. He shifted his upper body a little so he could drape his arm over the back of the chair. Just as Papa does. I thought to myself, it's a young man with gestures like these that Mama fell in love with. In a flash, I saw them again, Papa and her, in their wedding clothes, framed on the living-room wall. Oddly enough, the two of them were still there, still gazing at one another with hopeful eyes. People's lives might be ruined at any time, but pictures resisted the onslaught. They trapped us forever in sentimental remembrance. Or else inspired us to be crazy enough to start over again.

Was Michael in love? It hardly mattered. One day he would be, he was bound to take his place on a white wall, which would yellow along with the photograph. Other pictures would gradually swarm around it, snapshots of children, dark-haired little girls growing ever more graceful and well-behaved until one night, when nothing unusual was supposed to happen, the truth would break, like a windowpane shattered by a stone. Then there would be other photos of Michael on the wall in yet another house, they'd be surrounded by snapshots of other children. But how could I be so sure? I didn't know anything about him. For now, Michael was listening with the typical enthusiasm of a twenty-seven-year old, while Jean-Bernard went on and on about how the office was run. That wink he gave me when Michael retrieved some document from his briefcase — it whisked me back into the presence of the Jean-Bernard of Jérôme's time, the man who'd been brimming with energy, plans, wonderful ideas. Just looking at the two of them, you could picture the future. After his training period, Michael would stay on, he would take my place. The wheel would keep turning, I could leave without any worries.

When do you plan to leave? Michael jumped. I explained immediately that nobody knew, he was the first one in the family to hear about it. Michael smiled. Because of the word *family*, I thought. I blushed. I felt I was going back on what I'd done, I had expended so much effort to detach myself from Papa. I now disowned that, and Michael saw it. So did Jean-Bernard. To create a diversion, I quickly answered the question, I would leave as soon as possible, it all depended on the excavations at Carthage, the contracts at the office. The apartment. I hadn't found anyone yet. Perhaps Michael, if he stayed on. I would rent out my home to him at a ridiculously low price, I'd be able to leave with an easy mind. But I was dreaming, things never sorted themselves out quite so easily. *One can't have everything.* Mama's phrase. Just for a moment I clenched my jaws. A phrase for the weak, for losers. But during the past few days it had suddenly sounded different. Whenever I said, *I'm going away*, everything I was leaving behind took on a strange beauty. The river, now freed from its sheets of ice, boats flying foreign flags, the bustling city, golden in the sunlight, the city I loved the way one loves a character in a novel. Every time, I needed to reconcile myself to giving it up. Could Michael understand?

With his charming accent, he said, *I love challenges*. I smiled a little too eagerly. He might not have any Martin blood flowing in his veins, but Michael was just like me, he belonged to the race of warriors. And yet, one day, a drawbridge would collapse, or a tower, he'd lose his buoyant self-confidence, feel very small beneath his armour, let others take over the fighting. He would do as I do, he would leave.

10

Michael studies the faces printed on the tiny rectangles. He's pensive, surprised, shocked at seeing Papa's arm wrapped around Mama's waist. He knew, of course, but words aren't the same as pictures. Here he actually sees Papa's gaze, Papa's gesture, Papa's whole body reaching out for a woman who doesn't look like his own mother. There's also what you can imagine, gestures too intimate to be photographed. Perhaps he'll get up from his chair, throw the photos into the fireplace. As I did with Jasmina's picture. How do I know that in Rome my jealousy won't return, violently sometimes, along with my anxiety? Then Dominique's indignation will come on top of Mama's worry, how crazy to follow a man who hasn't forgotten!

Michael has put the photos down on the little table, he picks up one of the Phoenician gods, murmurs, *You'd think it was a Giacometti.* It's not a question, more a statement, while he caresses the bronze statuette. What is going through his mind right now? Is he wondering if there's any room left for him to be creative after so many civilizations? I stare at his fingers, long fingers, much more beautiful than Alessandro's, who has the hands of a farmer. But they're fingers that can caress a woman. Michael sets the poor Phoenician god down again among his own kind, in the unfamiliar world of the little table.

Will Michael feel like a fish out of water in Montreal? He swears he won't — already as a teenager he wanted to leave, as Richard had. His words hit me like a slap. I react, with the voice of my vengeful days, *Papa didn't leave, he abandoned us, Mama, Anna, and me.* I can't get a hold of myself, I'm trembling, I blurt things out — the scene in the restaurant, Mama's collapse, Anna's pain, and the weight, the immense weight, the weight of the world that rested on my shoulders.

Michael has huddled himself up in Alessandro's armchair, his head bent down towards his hands, he looks like a shamefaced little boy. He is probably trying to stick back together the pieces of the picture I've just torn up, *his* father is not the man *I* knew, I'm sure that's what he'd tell me if I were willing to listen. A siren cuts through the silence of the room, ambulance, police, or fire engine — I shudder, as if, nearby, my anger had caused another tragedy. I manage to get a grip on myself, I say, *I'm being harsh, aren't I?* He nods. But he doesn't try to defend Richard Martin, the Anglophone I barely know. He enters his childhood, lays it out before me. I see tiny, insignificant events emerging. A man is trotting along behind a little boy, he is taking him to a hockey game, gives him a dog for his birthday. And that little boy moves me, I don't know why. He lives on a different planet, with arenas and the love of a dog he treats like a pal. No jealousy, no twinges in my stomach. On *my* planet there were cats, one tawny cat after another, and acting lessons, and the plays Papa performed in.

Michael's eyes grow wide, he had no idea Papa used to act, he just can't imagine it, and I can't imagine that he didn't know, probably Eileen doesn't either, Papa must have left all his roles right here when he made his exit. Was it Michael who wanted to see the photos of Papa when he was *my* father? We ended up sitting side by side on the sofa, poring over my childhood. A small beige-brick house on a quiet street, a church for my first communion, a primary school, we were looking at a little girl just like all the other little girls of the neighbourhood, except for one detail — an aunt popping up here and there in all her glorious madness.

Who is that? Michael asks. It suddenly dawns on me, Michael has never seen Anna, never been involved in her life. He wants to hear about her, I try to describe the events in an orderly way. I should sort out the years, the treatments, and say, *before* or *after* she was hospitalized. I just can't do it. So I open the old photo-albums. There, Anna is a lovely young girl whom I never knew. I never knew the little boy she is holding on her lap either. Nor the dog beside them. *He's like mine*, says Michael. I merely smile, caressing the little boy with my finger. Perhaps we are only capable of forgiving a child.

11

Your mother didn't cry as she waved her handkerchief in the Rome railway station. Elsa held her by the arm, *she* was going to stay, she would marry a boy who lived on your street, find an apartment close to the house where you'd both been raised. Already in childhood it was quite clear — you were protected, Alessandro. Sofia Moretti would follow your journey on the map you'd left with her, the train, then the boat all the way to Tunis. One day she, too, would sail for Tunis. You would recognize her dark form on the deck of the ship. When you kissed her, you would notice a tiny teardrop at the corner of her eyes. And her black dress, a new dress exactly like all the others she had painstakingly sewn by the feeble lamplight.

For one brief moment I lowered my eyes, I pictured my own mother at the Fiumicino airport, luminous in a tangerine dress, her favourite colour. Huddled up inside her urn, Anna could no longer serve as a pretext. Boredom would set in, a dizzying boredom. Mama would get up, head off to the travel agency where she used to buy tickets to go down south, she would decide on the dates, ask her neigbour to feed the cat, she would leave her native soil. I'd be looking out for her the way one looks out for one's mother.

A red dot began shimmying in the distance and I opened my eyes wide. Already the Spanish-style inn, what architect could possibly have agreed to design such a building? In an hour, the bus would be driving onto the big bridge, then came the moment of truth. Mama would be waiting for me at the station, we'd go to a restaurant, I finally had to say to her, *I'm leaving.*

I wasn't able to keep quiet until the coffee came. Two lovers kissed and, without thinking, I ran my finger over my lips, I uttered the first word, then the second, the others followed, I kept on talking, the sounds airily chased one another like summer clouds. One could come and go without the image of disaster looming up every time in the words' silvery surface. I poured it all out, the need to love and be loved, the need to believe, the urge to live life to the fullest. I talked as we do when a window opens and we can suddenly glimpse joyful love, the kind that pulls us towards the light.

I hope you've made the right decision. Was she worried, or was this a veiled reproach? I turned my eyes towards the bay window, it seemed almost impossible to believe that galaxies might blaze into view in the monotonous expanse of pale, empty sky. And yet, all we needed to do was imagine nighttime, all we had to do was look beyond the blue, to see the fabulous things we're told about in books. I didn't try to defend myself. I said, *I'd like you to come and visit me at my place in Rome.* On the tabletop, I unfolded the map, I pointed out where Alessandro lives, then the Forum, and the Coliseum, I asked, *Wouldn't that be just like going over my history lessons together when I was a schoolgirl?* I'd said exactly the right thing to win her over, she gave me a radiant smile. My mother is a believer. She only believes in the past, but she does believe.

12

He was expecting me. Alessandro's voice sounded resolute, deceptively jolly, he was trying to cover up his unhappiness. Yet every now and then it would surface in the strong emphasis he put on certain syllables. I happened to catch sight of my reddened, puffy eyes in the mirror. If Alessandro had been here, he would have seen the little bags under my eyes, the dark circles, the fine lines. In fifteen or twenty years, they would be wrinkles, I would look like Mama. I felt no apprehension, Mama's wrinkles were attractive. Once again I heard, *I'm expecting you*, in a tender, anxious tone, and I answered, *Yes*. I had been turned down for the Prix de Rome, but I would leave anyway.

I could have recited the letter. My application hadn't been accepted, the large number of submissions had made the jury's task difficult, they were sorry. I crumpled the sheet of paper into a ball, tossed it into the fire. It bounced about for a moment before being consumed by the flames. Soon it would be part of the ashes, the last of the season. This fall, it would be Michael who'd get the fire going again, not me. Papa and Eileen would be sure to come, they'd sit on my sofa, Papa would get up to rearrange the logs in the hearth, I would betray Mama. But was it a real betrayal?

Darkness already submerged the room. I turned on all the lights to keep away the ghosts. No matter how often I repeated to myself, what are you afraid of? my hands were shaking, I just didn't feel reassured. I hadn't got the Prix de Rome, yet I was leaving — one year, hardly the end of the world, after that we would see, perhaps we'd feel like coming back. What was I so afraid of? I thought about Alessandro's Phoenicians who travelled on their small ships to the very end of the known seas. I thought about my father's great-grandfather, a Martin, and about a woman whose name I don't know, perhaps they'd kissed for the first time by the mast of a large sailing ship, what had they just left behind? A country, a mother, a profession, or debts, a criminal record, an unbearable life. All of them, things one could only surmise. And fear, I'm sure, the dizzying fear of coming back to a land of ice, terror, the same stark terror that was spreading through me once again this evening like an incurable hereditary illness.

13

Miraculously, this morning, it was summer. I knew it the instant I opened my eyes. An almost fierce kind of light forced its way through the blind, the enormous clouds massed in yesterday's sky had been driven away. Everyone at the office turned out to be in a November mood, except for Michael who was all excited about heading off to a building site with Marc to meet the contractor. Jean-Bernard whispered in my ear, *Such splendid enthusiasm!* I smiled a little wistfully — on what building site had I lost my own enthusiasm? But I would find it again in the ruins of Rome, the monuments, the blending of styles and materials. I would carry out my project even though I hadn't got the prize, I would see it through because I believed in it. Like the woman with the perfect lips who watched over the museum.

You couldn't see those lips from here. I flung open the French doors and stepped out barefoot onto the balcony. If I peered into the blue in front of me, would I see the smile of the unknown woman in empty space again? Exactly a year ago she threw herself off her balcony, but the anniversary of a suicide isn't something you call attention to. At least I'd be thinking about her. Tonight, Fanny and I would raise our glasses, we'd celebrate her first poems being published in a magazine. Would she give a thought to her aunt? Far be it from me to remind her. Fanny was vibrantly alive. She was starting university, she had already begun preparing for her trip to Rome, she'd come with Étienne, if they were still in love.

The other night, a merry group met up in Alessandro's dining room, Fanny, Étienne, Jean-Bernard, Mama, and also Michael, and Papa, and Eileen, yes, Eileen — her presence there seemed the most natural thing in the world, I shuddered at the thought when I woke up. I saw this dream as a premonition. Perhaps Papa would take it into his head to visit me in Rome, who knows? Alessandro laughed when I described the scene to him, Rome had known so many turnabouts. I smiled, was it Jasmina's death, Alessandro's age, the war, or having spent his life kneeling in the red earth of Carthage — what had transformed Alessandro into a man always ready to forgive? Nothing had worked for *me*, the spirit of forgiveness hadn't stirred in my breast. Yet I did muster up the courage to telephone Toronto. So far, Michael had held his tongue, but he could easily blurt something out, and that would be a slap for Papa, for Eileen too, how would Alessandro react if he found out through Marco that Gianni was moving to New York? He'd be hurt, and so would I, on his behalf.

Papa never opened his mouth, he was like one of those Phoenician vases, its secret hidden away. But I braved his silence, I explained things as frankly as I could. Tunis, Montreal, Rome. Three names of cities, an open loop into which I shoved every-thing I wouldn't talk about. My own life. *I hope you'll be happy.* I said, *Yes*, looking hard at the tiny statuettes in the middle of the table. Why did my voice sound tearful when I hung up? I hadn't received anything, but I'd stopped expecting anything a long time ago. Here we were, the two of us, bound together by the same name, we did our best to fill the distance between us with suitable phrases, and that suited me just fine, I'd learned to feel this way. Yes, all my life that had suited me.

The phone began to ring. A glimmer of hope. Had Papa pulled himself together once he got over his surprise? I recognized Eileen's voice, she was delighted for me. I thanked her. This time, it was a genuine thank-you.

14

All day long I dreaded the moment, the hands of the clock plodding blindly on, drawn forward by the memory of the catastrophe. What would happen this evening, at the very moment when France had thrown herself into empty space? A scream so powerful it would engulf the city, we'd all disappear without a trace, like those small peoples who didn't have boats to flee in. I needed to keep busy. I picked out the vegetables one by one, bought cheeses that smelled of monasteries, paper napkins with wildly colourful prints, I wanted a beautiful meal, and flowers on the table, tonight there would be beauty. All afternoon I searched for beauty, so tonight I might see laughter on our lips, happy laughter that would burst the leaden cloud of fear.

Fanny arrived with her magazine and straightaway wanted me to read her poems, right there, on the printed page, in black and white. I plunged my nostrils into the fragrance of the fresh paper. I read while I tried to make the words resonate in my flesh. Her text was beautiful, I told her so. Dreamily she turned her small face towards the French doors, then she stated she would continue this year, she wanted to complete the collection, she'd bring it to me in Rome, it would be her Christmas present. Not a word about her aunt. She stared at a gap in the blue sky, and there were no lips that smiled as they fell. She was able to forget. Fanny resembled Alessandro. In Rome, the apartment had now been redecorated. On the walls, there were no more photographs of the old life, Jasmina would not be there when we lay snuggled up against each other in our large bed.

The kitchen is wonderfully messy. Empty wineglasses, tiny islands of dirt on the tablecloth, whole archipelagos, and that big coffee stain, an uncharted land jutting into the sea. If Alessandro had been here, he would have pieced together for Fanny the Phoenicians' territory all the way to the Atlantic Ocean, we would have followed his short, broad finger a little nostalgically as it slid over the table, the world has become so small, what is there left for us to explore? But Alessandro would have started to laugh, wasn't Jean-Bernard getting his youthful enthusiasm back because of Michael's eagerness? As for Étienne, he was mulling over another film script, and Mama would come to visit us, we'd surely manage to persuade her in the end.

Slowly the city falls silent. Now, all we hear is a distant murmur, a hum, a rolling tide, the sound of steady breathing, undisturbed by blaring car horns. Or the wail of an ambulance siren. In Rome, you must be up, Alessandro, you're working on a new article, or you're having your coffee on the balcony. In a little while you'll write, *Ti penso*, when I am dropping off to sleep. I wish you were here with us. We would have one last drink on the balcony, in total silence, dazzled by the arch of light gliding across the sky before it drifts off into worlds that will always be unknown to us. But never mind, we can't know everything. We would contemplate the night, we would map out possible journeys into the galaxies. All it takes is imagination.

about the translator

Liedewy Hawke's translation *Hopes and Dreams: The Diary of Henriette Dessaulles, 1874-1881* won the 1986 Canada Council Prize for Translation (now the Governor General's Award for Translation) as well as the John Glassco Prize. Her other translations include *Memoria* (Louise Dupré's *La memoria*), published by Simon & Pierre in 1999, and *House of Sighs*, a translation of Jocelyne Saucier's *La vie comme une image*, published by Mercury Press in 2001.